Read all about Justin Case in:

A *Kirkus Reviews* Best Book of 2010

An IndieBound Selection for Fall 2010

"The writing is sharp, unpredictably clever, and establishes third grade as a minefield of the absurd—which is to say, real life."—Avi, Newbery Medalist

★ "Vail employs easy, direct language in a rhythm and syntax that captures the essence of a charming, lovable, and very believable boy. Readers transitioning to longer fiction will groan, sympathize, and laugh out loud in delight. Absolutely marvelous."—*Kirkus Reviews*, starred review

"Honest and full of heart, *Justin Case* is a story for an oft-ignored segment of kids: the sensitive, introverted, and observant. The format will remind many readers of *Diary of a Wimpy Kid*, but with fewer illustrations and a more reflective tone than Jeff Kinney's series. This is subtly satisfying storytelling."—*School Library Journal*

JUSTIN CASE

Shells, Smells, and the Horrible Flip-Flops of Doom

By **Rachel Vail**

Illustrated by **Matthew Cordell**

FEIWEL AND FRIENDS

New York

I am deeply indebted to the many teachers, librarians, parents, and kids who so generously share their thoughts and ideas with me about Justin and his world. My sincere thanks go to Carin Berger, Mary Egan and all the Toribios, Amanda Kouzis, Meg Cabot, Magda Lendzion, Amy Kissel and Eli, Carol Brown, Janet Jackson, and especially, always, Eileen and Jeff Vail. Merle Oxman and I invented Camp GoldenBrook when we were 11; its inclusion here is my small tribute to her enduring spirit. Massive thanks to everyone at Feiwel and Friends, especially Liz and Jean, for all their meticulous attention and boundless enthusiasm, and to Amy Berkower for her guiding wisdom. My undying admiration and gratitude belong to Matt Cordell, who can bring so many complex feelings to sparkly life with a squiggly line. Finally, my appreciation is beyond measure for the three men who live with me and teach me by example about courage, joy, imagination, stinkiness, gummy candy, the superpower of full-out laughing together, and the perfection of love. —R.V.

A FEIWEL AND FRIENDS BOOK
An Imprint of Macmillan

To Zachary—R. V.

To Liz Szabla—M. C.

JUSTIN CASE

Shells, Smells, and the Horrible Flip-Flops of Doom

June 20, Sunday

Ahhhh.

Summer vacation started yesterday. That means for the next 79 days, including today, I have absolutely nothing to worry about.

Nothing to Worry About might be tied with gummy worms as my favorite thing ever.

I gave Dad gummy worms, a full half pound minus one or possibly two worms, for Father's Day. Nothing to Worry About is not a thing you could wrap even if you had excellent wrapping skills and a lot of tape. Gummy worms were challenging enough. Also I don't think Dad really worries anyway.

He seemed to like the gummy worms and didn't mind that they came from his own store. He probably shared just because he is nice, not to get rid of them.

But I have Nothing to Worry About all for myself, so even though I am not a father, it kind of felt like today was my day, too.

~~~~~

June 21, Monday

I used to be a worried kid. Back then, going barefoot would have given me a lot of thoughts like, *What if I step on a rusty nail or a sharp piece of glass or dog doo,* or *what if that's not actually blades of grass under my bare feet but really hundreds of slithering snakes?*

Today when I was barefoot, playing tag with my little sister Elizabeth, I mostly didn't think those kinds of thoughts very much at all.

It is much more relaxing to be this way.

Though dog doo would be so disgusting to step in with bare feet, I had to put my sneakers back on after a few minutes.

~~~~~

June 22, Tuesday

We pressed SEND on the Camp GoldenBrook sign-up page after I said "Yes, I am sure" about a thousand times.

I am sure.

At Science Camp, where I went last year and the year before, there's no pool and the only sport is tag. Which is optional, and also you do fun variations like Molecule Tag or Electron Tag. There is no Electron Tag at Camp GoldenBrook. There's Baseball and Basketball and Swim a Mile.

That is why Camp GoldenBrook is where all the runny-aroundy kids go. And none of the nice calm worried kids. I am not a worried kid anymore, but I am still not a runny-aroundy kid.

But I'm ready for Camp GoldenBrook. I *am* sure.

I would be more sure though if Mom and Dad would please stop saying, "Are you sure, Justin?"

~~~~~~~

June 23, Wednesday

My second-best friend, Noah, and his mom came with us to the town pool today. The problem with going to the town pool is that the moms want us out in the sun, but then they slather us with protection from it.

"If we could just stay inside, we'd be perfectly safe," Noah pointed out.

"What are we going to do with you guys?" Noah's mom asked us.

I didn't know the answer to that. So I just squinched up my eyes to keep the sunblock out of them and waited for Noah's mom to move on to a different subject.

"Can we go to the snack bar now?" Noah asked. He is good at changing the subject. Also at eating.

"If you take Elizabeth," Mom said, and gave me two dollars. "And put on your flip-flops."

We had to walk slowly to the snack bar because my feet are not used to flip-flops. The first time I wore them, this morning, I fell down, twice, on our deck. If I fall down at camp, it will be Very Bad. But Mom says I will get used to it. That is what she says about all the bad stuff, like cooked carrots and icy ocean water. And I never do. I am not somebody who gets used to it, which she should know by now. But she doesn't. I have to keep these flip-flops.

I like soft socks with lots of cushioning and no pinchiness or seams, and then my sneakers. My feet like to have some privacy. Flip-flops are barely even shoes, just bottoms and a pole to annoy the space between my big toes and the other guys. And too much air on my feet feels freaky, like I forgot to get all the way dressed.

On our way to there, Elizabeth told us about her plans for when she grows up. She is going to be an artist and a toll collector and a vegetarian.

"You don't like to eat meat?" Noah asked her.

"Yes, I do," she said.

"She thinks a vegetarian is an animal doctor," I explained.

"That's a veterinarian," Noah tried, even though I shook my head. I looked up at the whiteboard listing the snacks and wondered if anybody ever actually ordered a lime popsicle.

"No," Elizabeth said. "A veterinarian is somebody who fought in a war. That is why there's Veterinarian's Day."

"Don't even try," I warned Noah. "Trust me."

"I should know," Elizabeth said. "I am the one who is going to be a Vegetarian, not you."

"True," Noah said. "And a toll collector?"

"You stand in the booth and people give you money for

nothing! And then I can use all that money to buy more animals to be the doctor of! Cherry popsicle, please."

"I'll have a rainbow popsicle, please," I told the teenager behind the counter.

"Don't worry about Camp GoldenBrook, Justin," Noah said to me. "You probably won't get badly hurt or beat up."

"Thanks, Noah," I said. "What's that smell?"

"Summer," Elizabeth said.

"And if it's terrible, maybe you could switch back to Science Camp," Noah told me, and then smiled up at the teenager. "May I have a lime popsicle, please?"

After we finished, Mom said Noah and I should get in the pool and swim already, but we couldn't. You have to wait half an hour after you eat something or you could drown

because, possibly, you get too heavy or else something to do with cramps.

Noah is full of facts about ways you might die.

~~~~~~

June 24, Thursday

Luckily it rained today so the plan for me to go to the town pool with Xavier Schwartz and his babysitter and my horrible flip-flops got canceled.

Xavier Schwartz has gone to Camp GoldenBrook since kindergarten.

He is practically king of the runny-aroundy kids and probably an excellent swimmer, too. He seems like somebody who would hold somebody's head underwater as a joke, even though that is Not Funny. Xavier Schwartz was my enemy until third grade, and maybe he still is, or maybe he's one of my best friends. He is the kind of friend who is a little scary and hard to decide about, like maybe that was a friendly hug he was giving me or maybe that is called beating me up. My muscles tighten whenever Xavier Schwartz comes near me.

Sometimes rain is just what a day needs.

~~~~~~

June 25, Friday

It doesn't get dark out these days until practically bedtime. That makes it really hard to wind down.

I am sitting on my bottom bunk, still winded very up. I had to get a cup of water because I was desperately thirsty. Then unfortunately I had hiccups. Noah says the best way to get rid of hiccups is to swallow a teaspoon full of sugar.

Apparently in our family we don't do that.

When the hiccups finally went away, I had to go to the bathroom. I could not help that. While I was there, I noticed a mosquito bite that needed some stuff sprayed on it. I'm sorry if that is inconvenient for some people like Mom, who was very busy cleaning up from our day—*for goodness' sake, Justin, enough already*—but it was itching my arm off.

The most recent time that Dad said, *Good night, Justin*, it sounded more like, *Good NIGHT, Justin*.

So now I can't call them again, or they will start yelling their heads off at me even though the ticking sound I keep hearing could be The Boiler downstairs in our basement, which might explode all of our pipes any second.

If it does, I probably will not be able to go to Camp GoldenBrook due to injuries.

My first summer of Camp GoldenBrook, which I am SO looking forward to. And I might miss the whole thing because of getting blown up into a thousand pieces by The Boiler, which is a very mean-looking thing that has fire in it and is very dangerous. Dad even said so when I was banging on it when I was little, and I have not forgotten.

Maybe it would be best for me to suggest to them that probably a very dangerous thing should not be in our basement doing that ticking and possibly other dangerous stuff. And they could call the Boiler Removers right now or the cops.

But no, I am not yelling downstairs to my parents to call 911 for this emergency. It is their own fault if we all blow up. I just hope I am making a wise decision, unlike the one I made about my new sneakers.

I actually first liked the velvety-textured brown ones that looked cozy and calm. Mom said those looked nice, but on the other hand the white ones with silver looked fast and good for sports. I wanted to be good at sports and very fast, so I said okay to the white-and-silver sporty sneakers.

The rest of today whenever I looked down, I thought some other kid's feet got stuck on the bottoms of my legs.

So I think maybe I made a bad choice at the shoe store today, and now maybe I am making another bad choice by not warning Mom and Dad even though I hear The Boiler ticking.

If it really is The Boiler, which it probably isn't.

Just in case it is The Boiler and it is about to explode because it is very dangerous (or maybe a bad guy tinkered with it because of Evilness) and we are all going to blow up, I have gathered up all my best stuffties to shield them from the explosion. We are squishing together in the far corner of my lower bunk bed where we evacuated to because you would not want to be on the top bunk in a Boiler Explosion, I think. Or maybe the top would be better. But I have no time to change that now. I am just going to stay right here on the bottom bunk, on top of all of these very worried and slightly smooshed stuffties. I am trying not to drip tears on anybody. I am a brave kid, now. Not a worried kid. I will protect these stuffties if it is the last thing I do.

The Boiler keeps ticking.

TICK TICK TICK

Or it might be Dad's watch. He might have taken it off when he added cool water to my too-steamy bath earlier and the cold-water-turny thing was screwed on too tight for me to adjust it with my soapy hands. Maybe Dad left his watch in the bathroom, which is right next to my room. It could definitely be Dad's watch that is ticking, which would be good.

Except for the still having to go to Camp GoldenBrook in sneakers that don't look like they could possibly be my sneakers if I don't blow up problem.

~~~~~

June 26, Saturday

I guess it wasn't a bomb because nothing seems to have blown up.

Well, except for possibly Qwerty.

He woke us all up by making sounds like a truck honking. Mom asked him, "What's wrong, Qwerty? What's wrong?" He looked up at her with his big sad dog eyes like, *I have no idea, lady. Something crazy.*

And then, *boom*. He exploded. Well, kind of. It was a barf explosion. Dog puke everywhere.

It looked like he puked a rainbow.

"What did you eat, Qwerty, you crazy dog?" Dad asked him.

Qwerty's answer was just more rainbow-colored dog puke.

〰〰〰

June 27, Sunday

Gummy worms.

Dad apparently had a little snack Friday night after everybody else went to bed, and then left the half-full bag of gummy worms I gave him for Father's Day out on the couch.

We found the last few half worms and the chewed-up paper bag under the couch this morning.

The heads of both Dad and Qwerty hung down low while

Mom had a little chat with the two of them about inappropriate snacking.

∿∿∿∿∿

June 28, Monday

"Come on, Justin," Mom said, holding up a bunch of swimsuits with tags hanging off them. "Camp GoldenBrook starts next week."

"Mmm-hmm," I said. I was in the middle of a battle with the new knights my grandparents sent me, so I could not really pay attention right then.

"Try these on, please," Mom said. "Right now, Justin."

The Dragon Green Walker was in a battle to death against the best good guy, Achilles Heel. Also, I hate trying on clothes. She made me anyway.

And then Mom did not say, *I am proud of you, Justin, for trying on these scratchy swimsuits that have tags poking at your hip skin and weird netting all inside them, which is very tickly on your private parts, right in the middle of an epic battle, which the good guy lost because of the bathing-suit catastrophe, so civilization is now doomed.*

No. She did not say any of that.

What she said was that we are going to have to get onto a good schedule because Camp GoldenBrook is the kind of camp that you have to take a yellow bus to. Every day. And it is also the kind of camp that you don't get home from until 5 P.M.

Science Camp, which I went to last year and the year before, was only until 3 P.M. And the moms bring you and pick you up. And no swimming/no swimsuits.

So maybe the suits I said were good are not. I have no experience with choosing which swimsuits fit me right or are good. Mom always made those decisions independently, in the past. These might be too small, and they'll be pinchy and embarrassing or too big and fall off in the pool. Or just be ugly.

But it is too late now. The tags are off.

Even the horrible mighty Dragon Green Walker looked a little serious about what a mess I have gotten myself into.

~~~~~~

June 29, Tuesday

Mom was sighing as she looked at the website of Camp GoldenBrook. She asked me the question again of "Are you sure you are up to this camp, Justin?"

I gave her the answer again of "Yes, I am sure."

Dad winked at me and called me Atta Boy, which is his name for me when he is proud of me. Then he asked me if I knew who Gerta was.

I didn't.

Gerta is apparently a poet *and* a guy.

He wrote the poem "Be bold, and mighty forces will come to your aid."

That is it. That's the whole poem, and it doesn't even rhyme. But the poor guy's name was the girl's name of Gerta, so maybe he was trying to reassure himself in the poem. Maybe he was hoping mighty forces would come to his aid if only he was bold enough to write one-line poems that don't rhyme or have nature words in them, and admit he had a girl's name. Or maybe he hoped the forces would be mighty enough to change his name to a boy name.

"That's a cool poem," I told Dad, because he was waiting all hopeful with his eyebrows up near his hair. "I like that. 'Be bold . . .' "

" 'And mighty forces will come to your aid,' " Dad said again, smiling. Then he grabbed me by the neck and hummed into my hair. Sometimes Dad tells me stuff like poems that don't rhyme and then grabs me by the neck and hums at the

top of my hair. Maybe when I get old and
have kids, I will be weird like that, too.

After that I thought maybe Dad would
want to play with me, the game of my
choice, since he was so proud of me and I
listened nicely to his poem that didn't
rhyme by a girl-man, but no.

I am not sure why Dad has to sew name tags into all my
stuff instead of playing Battleship with me. Nobody will be
able to read my last name anyway. It is Krzeszewski. Even we
can't read it.

Everybody used to call me Justin K., even after Justin R.
moved away to Alaska before second grade. But then in third
grade, Xavier Schwartz said that I was the most worried kid in
the world because I thought we should use pencils before the
markers on our map-drawing project *just in case* we mess up.

I am not a worried kid anymore, but I still don't think
that was even a particularly worried thing, compared to most
of my worried thoughts. It didn't seem to me like pencil first
was such a crazy idea. But to Xavier Schwartz it did. He said
instead of Justin K., my name should be Justin Case.

Pretty soon everybody at school was calling me Justin Case instead of Justin K. I don't know if everybody at camp will, too. Maybe I could get a better nickname there like Ace or Spike or Sharkey. Maybe if we had ordered name tags that instead of Justin Krzeszewski said, *Justin, whose nickname is actually Ace, so please call him that* or *Justin "Spike" Krzeszewski* I would have a better shot at a cool nickname.

But maybe not. We may as well be playing Battleship anyway because nobody will even see those name tags. Dad is sewing them on the *insides* of my clothes.

~~~~~~~

June 30, Wednesday

The reason there are now name tags *inside* all my clothes is:

We have to take off our clothes at Camp GoldenBrook.

I looked up the camp website and downloaded the schedule while Mom and Dad thought I was playing my half hour of computer games. I didn't copy it down, but I remember the basic idea of the schedule. It was:

Go to camp.

Take off clothes and silver sneakers.

Put on swimsuit and flip-flops.

Get wet and cold in the pool.

Take off swimsuit and flip-flops.

Put on clothes and silver sneakers.

Get sweaty doing rough sporty stuff.

Eat in the "mess hall" (whatever that is, but it does not sound like a place anybody would want their food to be).

Take off clothes and silver sneakers.

Put on second swimsuit and same old horrible flip-flops.

Get cold and wet again.

Take off swimsuit and flip-flops.

Put on clothes and silver sneakers.

Do more boring sweaty sports that require skills.

Sing.

Go home.

No wonder Mom had so many sighs coming out of her.

I somehow convinced my parents to send me to Clothes-Changing Camp. And it starts in five days. I have to work on my courage a little bit more, I think. Also changing without letting anything private show. Also maybe sports skills, eating messes, and flip-flop walking without ending up on my face.

〰〰〰

July 1, Thursday

I hate summer break.

It goes too quickly.

I've hardly done anything, and here we are already partway into July. The days are just flying by.

~~~~~~

July 2, Friday

Xavier Schwartz and Gianni Schicci came over for a double playdate today.

They have both been to Camp GoldenBrook before. They said it is the best camp and so much fun and basically all you do is play all day. You have to hold your towel in your teeth and just change behind it—no big deal. The counselors are awesome and teach the kids songs with bathroom words in them and sneak us extra cookies. I am so happy I made the decision to go there. I love playing and cookies, and probably I will also start to enjoy songs with bathroom words, too.

After we had a battle with my knights and talked about how awesome camp is going to be, we made up a game called Houdini. Two of us would tie the other one up using Elizabeth's jump rope and hair bands, the blanket from my top bunk, and Dad's weights, which we attached to the hair bands at the feet. Xavier and I tied up Gianni and covered him with a blanket. Then we left the room to see how long it would take for him to get out.

It took a long time.

We thought maybe he died.

But he didn't.

Then we had a snack.

～～～～

July 3, Saturday

My little sister Elizabeth is so excited she might burst open like a whacked piñata, she says.

"You are a whacked piñata," I said.

"Justin," Mom said.

Elizabeth can't wait for Art Camp to start on Monday. She already packed her yellow-and-blue camp bag with no swimsuits or flip-flops, just markers and colored pencils and a snack in it. She is going to sit next to her boyfriend Buckey at lunch and sing silly songs they make up together. She already started one. It's called "I Am a Whacked Piñata, a Whacked Piñata, a Whacked Piñata."

When she was younger, Elizabeth was scared of everything, and I had to comfort her. Now I sometimes accidentally wish she could be a gerbil instead of a sister.

~~~~~~

July 4, Sunday

We went to watch the fireworks at the high school with my grandparents, who brought me two more more knights, each with a matching horse, when they came over. They are

22

excellent grandparents except for the little problem of what happens when we go to the fireworks. It is the same thing every year.

Gingy, my grandmother, keeps yelling, "Ooooh!" or "Ahhhh!" or "That was the best one!"

And Poopsie, my grandfather, says, "I think that was the Grand Finale!" after every single firework, even the first one.

∿∿∿∿

July 5, Monday

When we got home last night, there was a big surprise.

I thought we had been robbed by a dangerous criminal.

Dad said no.

It turns out Qwerty, who is huge and slobbery and scary strong enough to drive away any bad guys, is terrified of fireworks.

I understand about being terrified. I used to be terrified of a lot of things. I used to be afraid of food that jiggles, bad guys, teachers who are yellers, one of my stuffties (Snakey), death, one of my friends (Xavier Schwartz), and dogs, including Qwerty. Now I am not completely terrified of any of those things.

Just partially terrified.

Well, I am still completely terrified of death and Jell-O.

But what I do when I am terrified is hide in my bed and scrunch up as small as possible.

What Qwerty did when he was terrified is tear open the garbage and also the couch and redecorate them all over the entire house.

So today I could not spend the day getting good at sports for camp, which starts tomorrow.

Instead, I had to spend it playing with Qwerty in the backyard because he was so freaked out by the rug shampooer Mom had to rent from the hardware store to clean up the mess he had made. When she turned it on, Qwerty started yelping while running around in tight circles, chasing his tail and trying to bite it.

"He is going to eat himself up!" Elizabeth screamed, and started crying and yelping, too. "He is going to gobble up his tail, and then his legs and body and . . ."

"Justin," Mom screamed, "take Qwerty and your sister OUTSIDE!"

Qwerty is very enthusiastic, but he doesn't get that in the

game of Fetch, it is the DOG who is supposed to go get the
stick, not the kid. So that didn't work. Also Elizabeth was still
running around in crazy circles until she fell down, which
made Qwerty bark even more and pay even less attention
to fetch.

It took a while and a few games of Time Machine to calm
them both down. I had to bring them to Colonial Virginia
and then a medieval village (where we slayed a dragon, played
by the big rock in the Way-Back of our yard) before we all
stopped running around in crazy circles.

Even those of us who were only running around in crazy
circles deep down on the hidden inside.

That rug shampooer thing really was horribly loud and

slightly terrifying, even though I would never admit it or be scared of it for real myself, too much.

I got to come inside when Xavier Schwartz called on the telephone. By then Mom was done with the machine and our house smelled weird, but I guess better.

Xavier said, "Hi Justin Case this is Xavier Schwartz."

"I know," I said.

"Um," he said. "Who are you sitting with on the camp bus tomorrow?"

"I don't know."

"Well, I'm sitting with Gianni Schicci."

"Oh."

"No offense. He's my best friend."

"I know."

"You can sit across the aisle from us," Xavier said.

"Okay."

"We'll save you a seat if we get on the bus first. If you get on first, you save us a seat."

"Okay."

"Well, bye."

"Bye," I said, and hung up. I didn't go outside to where

Elizabeth and Qwerty were stranded in a medieval village, waiting for me to come back. I know I promised them I would, but right then I really had to go lie down on my top bunk instead and just rest for a while. I wasn't worrying about who in the world I am going to sit with on the bus tomorrow morning because I am not a worried kid anymore.

It is a good thing I am not, too, because if I were, I would not be able to sleep all night tonight worrying about that thing I hadn't even realized would be a thing to worry about.

∿∿∿∿∿

July 6, Tuesday

I sat with Montana C.

She gets on the bus right before me. When I stepped up into the bus, she yelled from near the back, "Hey, Justin Case!"

"Hi," I said, and waved a little.

Heads of other campers popped out into the aisle to look at who in the world is named Justin Case. Apparently it was me.

So I just stood in the bus aisle for a little longer than

might have been necessary, having nickname thoughts, like instead of saying hi maybe I should have said, "No, it's me—Sharkey!"

But I didn't. I just stood there sort of smiling and waving weakly toward Montana C.

"I didn't know you were coming to Camp GoldenBrook, Justin Case," Montana C. yelled. "Awesome! Sit with me!"

So I did. Montana C. is the most popular and the most friendly girl in my whole grade at school. The seats in the bus were the kind where you can't see anybody in the other rows. That is my favorite kind of bus seat. We slumped down with our knees on the seat in front of us and saved the seat across from us for Xavier and Gianni.

"This is gonna be an awesome summer, don't you think?" she asked me.

"Yeah," I said, but my voice did a weird dance move during the "yeah," so it kind of sounded like maybe I was yodeling. I didn't want to seem odd, so I did another couple of yodels then, like sometimes I just yodel in my spare time. Montana C. seemed a little concerned about that new hobby of mine.

So then I stayed quiet the rest of the ride to camp.

And then the day just got worse from there.

~~~~~~

July 7, Wednesday

I am a Hawk.

That is the group name of the kids going into fourth grade. Our counselors are a beautiful teenager named Natalia and an ugly teenager named either Jay or James. When James or Jay or whatever his name is first smiled at us, it looked like he was actually just showing his fierce teeth. His voice sounded like

a mean dog growling. I think he said we Hawks better be the best group in camp, but I don't know really.

Because it just sounded like we were already in trouble.

I am not sure why we would already be in trouble. We just got off the bus. We were still holding our backpacks full of bathing suits and towels and name tags.

But Camp GoldenBrook is not like regular life.

There's no getting used to it—you have to jump right into the cold pool.

At lunch we took food off the platter with our grubby hands, which we didn't have to wash first. The food was called hockey pucks.

With full mouths, all the Hawks talked about the fact that we hate girls. Girls are so gross.

The boy next to me said, "You hate girls, don't you?"

I shrugged and said, "Duh. What do you think?"

"Yeah. Duh." He smiled. I guess I gave him the right answer.

The reason I was having a sweat attack and couldn't even eat my cookie after that is to me girls are actually still okay. Maybe I will stop liking them soon, but so far I can't.

And that was my first day of Camp GoldenBrook.

Well, that and also I had to run around so much and sweat and play sports without stopping except when you get knocked down and then you have to get right back up so much because people whose names are either James or Jay—and you don't know which—are shouting, "GET UP GET UP SHAKE IT OFF."

Yesterday and today, I fell asleep on the bus going home. The bus driver yelled my name to wake me up both times, which made the campers who were still on the bus laugh and laugh.

On the Camp GoldenBrook website, the campers' faces

looked calm and happy, rosy cheeked and sparkly. Not mean and mocking like those guys on the bus when I was blinking, trying to figure out what bad dream I was in the middle of. Not droopy and exhausted like mine when I got home and went straight to hide in the bathroom and not talk about how Camp GoldenBrook was going.

That is called false advertising, I think.

At dinner last night, Mom and Dad had gentle faces on when they asked how it went at camp. "Was it okay, Justy?" Mom asked.

She only calls me Justy when I am scared and unsturdy and need to be cuddled up. But I am not unsturdy anymore. I am rock solid.

So I picked up my head off the table and said, "It was fine. Fun."

"What are your counselors' names?"

"I don't know," I said. "May I be excused?"

"You okay?" Mom called after me.

I am doing fine. I can handle Camp GoldenBrook. I got through the second day today. I didn't throw up or fall asleep and drool on the long long long bus ride to camp or get hurt badly or chosen last for any game all day yesterday or today.

So everything is fine.

Kind of.

〰〰〰

July 8, Thursday

My Question: How is Newcomb not volleyball?

The Reason I did not ask my question: James or possibly his name is Jay says things like "Just shut up and play" to campers who ask questions. When James/possibly Jay talks, his nostrils flare out like his nose is a two-car garage.

So I will not be asking any questions this summer.

Anyway, I will be too busy changing my clothes. And trying not to keep getting hit in the head with balls of all colors and sizes. That is enough of a challenge for me apparently.

At first swim today, James/Jay shouted, "If you swam any slower, you'd be swimming backwards!"

I am not sure if he was yelling that at me or Gianni Schicci or some other random slow kid. It definitely wasn't Xavier or Cash, the new kid who hates girls. Xavier hangs around with that kid all day instead of Gianni—they are the two fastest Hawks.

Maybe it was Gianni he was yelling at. I know from being in class with Gianni last year at school that if a teacher is yelling a kid's name that name is pretty likely to be the name of Gianni. Occasionally it is the name of Xavier. It is almost never the name of Justin, which is the reason I am happy that my name is Justin.

So it probably wasn't me that the counselor was saying such a mean thing to.

Also there is no way a person, even a slow-swimming person, can swim backwards. I am pretty sure that is impossible. Which means the counselor James/Jay wasn't warning us of a danger. He was just being nasty. To kids. Even though he is supposed to be a counselor.

I do not think that is allowed, even at a place like Camp GoldenBrook.

I think he is a bad person, maybe.

Another bad thing is a food called hockey pucks for lunch in The Mess. They just call it The Mess. And that is a good name for that place.

First swim in the morning is Free Swim. That is very bad.

Changing in the locker room, standing barefoot and shivering on the cold concrete floor, even behind a towel bitten by my teeth and hanging down in front of me like a limp curtain is worse.

But swim test tomorrow is the winner of Worst Things.

Still, when Dad asked, "How was camp, Champ?" I said the lie, "Great."

The nickname of Champ is even better than the nickname of Ace or Sharkey and infinitely times better than the nickname of Justin Case. So that made it hard for me to complain. Somebody who has just been called Champ doesn't say, *I got water up my nose at swim,* and *The space between my big toes and my second toes is very sore from my horrible flip-flops,* and *I think maybe this camp is too rough for me.*

A person called Champ just says, "Great. Camp is Great!"

I am not so sure I will still be called Champ after the swim test tomorrow, so I have to enjoy it today while I can still get it.

∿∿∿∿∿

July 9, Friday

What I hate:

1. Changing clothes.

2. Biting into an apple bruise.

3. Swim tests.

4. The color red.

What I did at camp today:

1. Changed clothes.

2. Bit into an apple bruise.

3. Took a swim test.

4. Got into the group RED, which is the lowest group, also called Shallow.

What I did not do at camp today:

1. Get any of the pennies the awesome swim counselor named Mike threw into the shallow end, which is a very cool camp activity apparently.

2. Swim well enough to get into a good swim group.

3. Cry.

4. But it was close.

What I did not do after camp today:

1. Tell Mom and Dad about it.

∿∿∿∿∿

July 10, Saturday

We went to Gingy and Poopsie's beach condo. The reason I did not want to go swimming was not just because of the possibility of sharks in the ocean or grandmothers in the pool. I flat out needed one darn day off of swimming for goodness' sakes.

Also I think it should really be illegal to have a test in the summer. Poopsie is a lawyer so I might ask him later if I feel like telling anybody there was a swim test.

After Elizabeth swam the whole children's hours' time in the pool, we got kicked out of the pool area by the old man Gingy secretly calls Mr. Cranky Pants, and we all went down to the beach. Mom, Dad, and Gingy settled themselves on beach chairs to read. Poopsie decided we had no patience for nonsense like that. Poopsie said explorers like him and me and Elizabeth had to go on adventures.

We had to walk down the beach toward the ice-cream stand.

On our way, instead of discussing if summer testing of children is against the law in this country, we had a contest of jumping off the dunes. I got the farthest. Elizabeth got the complete forward-roll prize. Poopsie got the Funniest-Looking Dune Jump in History award.

Then we all got triple scoops.

So we all won.

On the way back, I found a tiny shell. It practically glowed

on the sand, like it had been waiting there for me. Elizabeth asked if she could have it, but I said no because it felt right away like this was my shell. I let her hold it, carefully, and then gave Poopsie a turn.

Poopsie let out a long whistle, admiring it.

"It's perfect," I whispered, taking it back.

"It is, Justin," Elizabeth whispered. "Perfect."

"It's not often you find a perfect thing," Poopsie said. "When you do, you'd better keep a hold of it."

"I will," I promised, more to my shell than to my grandfather.

I kept it in my hand the whole way back to the condo and didn't drop it or even drip any ice cream on it. I am not going swimming now even though it is afternoon kids' hours in the pool, because I am very busy admiring my shell and deciding where I am going to keep it from now on. Because this shell and I are going to stick together forever.

∿∿∿∿∿

July 11, Sunday

A kid should not have to explain why he just does not feel like swimming one weekend, even if it is beautiful out. Maybe there is no reason: He just would not like to swim, thanks anyway.

A thing I do not enjoy about blue skies and 82 degrees is that everybody is under pressure to be in a good mood even if they are not.

And they would maybe like to spend some time shooting bad guys in peace instead of swimming or kicking a ball.

When we picked up Qwerty from the kennel on our way home from the beach, he was so happy to see us he could not settle down. The whole way home in the car, he was telling us the story of his horrible weekend. We didn't understand the details because Qwerty talks only Dog. But we sure got the gist of it.

When he finally seemed done, I asked, "So you didn't have much fun at Doggie Camp, Qwerty?"

He looked me right in the eye like, *You have no idea what it's like in there!* And then he told me again the whole long story of his Weekend of Horror. Even though it was all in Dog, I could tell that it was full of sorrow and drool.

I knew just how he felt.

Because I was heading back to my camp in eleven hours.

～～～～

July 12, Monday

Quad is where everybody sings at the end of the day.

Some counselors play instruments like guitar and tambourine and ukulele. Some counselors do the songs in sign language while singing in English (or sometimes another language, possibly Spanish). The campers are all supposed to sing, no exceptions even if you have trouble with tune or don't know the words because last year you went to Science Camp instead.

But today it was too darn hot for me to sing. I tried for the first song, but I could not keep it up. My mouth and my eyes and my voice all needed to close down.

My favorite sport is just playing. The kind of playing where

you make up some imaginary things like bad guys or evil planets or demonic zombies, and then everybody chases everybody else around. At Camp GoldenBrook, there are no demonic imaginaries and there is no just playing. There are activities all day long.

I was so worn-out from activities and clothes changing and trying to walk in flip-flops when we go down to the pool and faking a cramp so I could get out early when my teeth were chattering that I had to lie down on my back right there in the middle of a song called "Baby Shark" instead of singing.

I truly didn't care if I got yelled at for the first time in my entire life.

While I waited to get yelled at, I watched the clouds sagging in the sky. They looked hot and tired, too.

The counselors were all too boiled to care if we participated, so nobody yelled at me, not even James/Jay.

Maybe this is how the tough kids get that way, I thought. They wear themselves out by so much activities, until their insides stop jangling with feelings.

Montana C. spread her towel next to mine, and I think she might have fallen asleep. I didn't want to look at her and have her ask me why I was looking at her. So I could not be certain if she was sleeping or just breathing slow and deep.

I also didn't want somebody else to notice me looking at Montana C. Like, for example, I didn't want Cash to see me looking at her and poke Xavier and say, *Look who likes Montana C.!* Cash calls her Montana C., even though there is no Montana B. at this camp because Montana B. went away to France for the summer to visit her grandparents, so Cash only knows one Montana (other than the state). But Montana C.'s name is just Montana C. It would be weird to call her Montana, even as a nickname, for short.

Cash doesn't know Montana B. because he is the new kid,

who moved here from Tennessee and says girls are gross in a cool slow accent. He is tall and has all his grown-up teeth, and he is the fastest Hawk. Also he is the most popular boy. Everybody answers yeah no matter what Cash says.

Xavier chose Cash as his buddy for free swim instead of his best friend, Gianni Schicci, today. Xavier and Gianni have been best friends since kindergarten.

Today Gianni spent a lot of time kicking rocks and growling. All because of this new kid Cash. Who I did not need teasing me about looking at Montana C. even to see if she was singing or sleeping or watching clouds like me.

So I just stayed still there on my towel with my eyes on the sky.

Quad is officially my favorite part of the Camp GoldenBrook day.

No progress on hating girls yet. But maybe hating girls is like tennis or Newcomb so it takes a lot of practice before you get good at it.

∿∿∿∿∿

July 13, Tuesday

James/Jay caught me laughing while we were making lanyards during the rainstorm. Apparently laughing is against the Camp GoldenBrook rules, like going barefoot to the pool even if your toe valley is rubbed raw from your horrible flip-flops. You have to wear them anyway, no excuses.

Also, apparently, no laughing.

Yesterday I thought I had grown out of minding if somebody puts me in trouble. Today I learned that maybe I didn't fully grow out of that. Also that the space between my big toes and my second toes is huge. I didn't ever know that about myself. Now all the Hawks do. It was the big attraction after first swim.

The reason I laughed at arts and crafts despite the recent

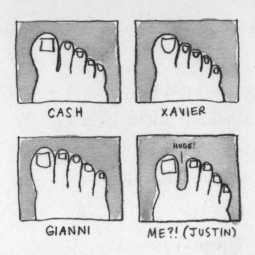

CASH

XAVIER

GIANNI

ME?! (JUSTIN)

toe-humiliation problem, which I have to complain about to Mom and Dad tonight for their lousy genes, is that when Xavier messed his lanyard up for the fortieth time, he made a snorty sound. It sounded exactly like a pig. Pigs make me laugh. Or, at least, pig sounds. I am not sure if an actual pig would be funny to me. I have never met an actual pig.

My guess is that I would find an actual pig less hilarious than a pig sound coming out of a kid. I might be a little bit scared of an actual pig. But I am not sure. Maybe I'd be brave.

James/Jay pointed his finger right at my nose.

"What's so funny, Funny Man?"

The reason I did not answer is because I normally do not get in trouble. Well, maybe sometimes with my parents.

But when somebody who is not Mom or Dad yells at me like that, I lose my word-forming skills. Also, when somebody calls me Funny Man in such an angry voice, it turns out, there is a chance I might start laughing.

I took a deep breath, the way Mom says I should when my feelings are knocking me around. While I breathed in, I wondered if I was more likely to laugh or cry on the out breath. It was about even, I decided.

"You are on my list," James/Jay growled at me while I was exhaling. That tipped me way more toward crying.

I didn't know counselors had lists. I still don't know what it means if you are on a counselor's list, or what to do about it.

I don't know if James/Jay counts as a kid or an adult or why he hates me. Usually, this kind of thing does not happen to me. Teachers often hate Xavier and Gianni so they are used to it. I have no skills for not minding this.

At lunch, we had hockey pucks again. I couldn't stab my teeth through the whatever it was, so I gave mine to Cash, who was very happy. Even though he is the opposite of chubby, he is always hungry. He said he has never been full in his life.

I keep thinking about that.

Then at Free Play after lunch I found out about a new game only a few boys are invited to play, and I got to be one of the special few now that I got in trouble (twice in one day) because of the toe-space/flip-flop issue and then the pig-noise issue. I used to just watch Bartholomew Wiggins play Parcheesi with Marcus Snoot-Slutsky during Free Play.

The new game is called Knuckles. It is a card game I don't know how to play. Cash said, "Just play, you'll get it. You're smart." I didn't want to say *not that smart*, *apparently*, but the truth is: I did not get it. All I know is that when you lose, you get hit with the side of the deck of cards right on your knuckles a number of times, with everybody counting up the hits together, in excited whispers. I lost four games and so did Gianni. Xavier lost twice and Koji three times. Cash lost zero times.

Knuckles is a secret game. You are not allowed to say the word *knuckles* to anybody, especially a grown-up. If you tell a grown-up, including parents or counselors, about the game of Knuckles, you are really going to Get It.

I am learning a lot of new things at this camp, like that

counselors have lists that they put kids on if they laugh at a pig noise and that counselors who are teenagers count as grown-ups even if they are mean to kids and that if you tell a grown-up that your friends hit you with a deck of cards if you lose a game you don't really know the rules of or if you even want to play, you will Get It.

I am hoping to learn some new things in the second half of July, like how to get off a counselor's list. I am also working on finger strength, so I can get out of the group of three Hawks (Bartholomew Wiggins, Penelope Ann Murphy, and me) who can't manage to stay up on those rings we have to swing across the mud puddles on. It would be nice to get at least one darn penny off the bottom of the pool, but maybe I am just too floaty to ever succeed at that. Also you have to open your eyes underwater, which I am never ever in my life going to do because I am not a fish so I don't have clear membranes protecting my eyeballs, and I don't care what the cool swim teacher Mike says—goggles do not keep the water out.

Another good ambition is if I could please figure out what the rules are of the game Knuckles so my fingers don't fall off from that, too.

I am hoping not to learn what "Get It" means or if there actually is quicksand under the mud puddles or why the juice at this camp is the type called Bug.

~~~~

July 14, Wednesday

July 14 is French for July 4.

Because of that, we had mini croissants for snack, and the counselors sang songs in French during Quad.

And Montana C. taught me how to say two things in French. One is *thank you* and the other is *shut up*. I can't remember which is which, though, so if I meet somebody French who gives me a nice thing, I will stay quiet, just in case.

I almost showed Montana C. my perfect shell, but then I didn't because Xavier yelled, "Hey, Justin Case!" so I had to go. I kept my hand in my pocket, rubbing the shell while I headed for the bus. My shell is the only thing that helps my aching knuckles.

Nothing helps the toes.

∿∿∿∿∿

July 15, Thursday

The only thing I could think of all through dinner was *Knuckles Knuckles Knuckles.*

I kept wondering what I should do if Mom asked, "What are those joints in the middles of fingers called?"

Then I almost said *knuckles* when Dad asked if I would like to go with him to get ice cream. I said, "Knuck—uhhh. Yes. Please. I would, yes, like to, yes. Okay. And that is all I have to say about that topic so please yes let's just go."

Dad looked at Mom like maybe she should call Dr. Carroll because maybe I had a fever or something.

Mom shrugged at him. That was her whole answer. And then, luckily, she did not ask what are those joints in the middles of fingers called? So I dodged the problem there for the moment.

I kept my jaw shut tight the whole drive to the ice-cream place and managed only to say, "Monster Cookie, please," instead of *knuckles* when Dad asked me what flavor I would like.

∿∿∿∿∿

July 16, Friday

On the way down to first swim, my left flip-flop broke apart. The sticky-uppy part came unattached from the bottom. My foot went slamming forward, and then I slanted so far backwards that I knocked right into Penelope Ann Murphy, and the two of us tumbled down the hill together.

The good news was we had to miss first swim.

The bad news was that she smelled like pudding and also the bleeding and the crying.

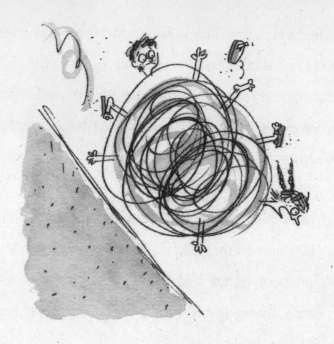

I mostly held mine in but Penelope Ann Murphy was not so successful with that. Then we had to go the nurse's office.

The nurse put Band-Aids on both my knees and gave me ice for my knuckles, which she noticed were red. She thought it was from the fall.

Penelope Ann stayed in the nurse's office the rest of the day, but I went back to the group after my counselor Natalia came to pick us up and gave us our clothes to change into. It was nice to change in the nurse's bathroom with the door closed, but it was really nice to walk alone with Natalia through the pine trees back to our group. I was secretly happy Penelope Ann Murphy needed some more time with the nurse. I tried to think of something witty and mature to say to Natalia. I considered saying, *Don't you think the pine trees smell sticky, but also smooth?* But then I thought maybe that wasn't so good.

My second idea was to say the poem of Be Bold and Mighty Forces Will Come to Your Aid, but I couldn't remember the poet's girl name. Marta? Golda? Also I wasn't sure how to start saying a poem. Just blurting it out like a burp did not seem like a good call.

Then I remembered that I had heard the swim counselor Mike say, "So far so good," to Natalia earlier in the week, and it made her laugh. It was a very sparky laugh. He also often says the word *whatevs*, which I think is short for *whatever*, but I am not completely sure.

So I was thinking maybe I could say, "So far so good," to Natalia, too, or possibly "Whatevs," if only she would please ask me something.

"So far so good" seems like a witty and mature thing to say to a beautiful teenager, so I had it at the ready.

"Whatevs" seems a little more risky. But she didn't ask me anything. "So far so good" and "whatevs" might be witty things but maybe less so just out of the blue. They should be a response. But somebody has to say something for even a witty response, or it's just weird.

And then there we were back with the Hawks at the field-hockey field.

"You okay?" Cash asked when I got there.

"So far so good," I said.

He smiled. "So far so good," he repeated.

"Yeah," I said. Everybody always says Yeah to Cash.

"Penelope, man. What is with that girl?"

I wasn't sure how to answer that so I said, "Yeah," again.

"She is so annoying."

"Yeah." I nodded. "Plus, she smells like pudding."

Cash cracked up at that. "Like pudding?"

"Yeah."

"Well, Pudding broke your flip-flops." He handed them to me.

"I hate these things anyway," I said, and chucked them off to the side of the field.

He laughed. He didn't even care that James/Jay was pointing at him. Then he picked me first for his team. My cut-up knees stopped hurting in the excitement of that. He picked me ahead of Xavier Schwartz.

But after a while, when the ball went merrily between my legs for the second time like I was making a tunnel for it, I had to sit out and rest them a bit. They were sore from the fall is why.

After Free Play and then Quad, my knees were better, but my knuckles were hurting a lot. I had to press them against the cool of the bus window the whole way home.

I don't know what I will tell Mom if she notices that they

are red. Mom is a very observant person. She could really notice that my knuckles are damaged and force me to tell her what the game of Knuckles is.

Maybe I could tell Mom my fingers are cold and just wear mittens so she won't suspect anything.

Because if she sees my knuckles are all so red, she will definitely force me to confess. She is also a very forceful person. Or she may just figure it out through Mother's Intuition, which I think is a thing they have that makes them know stuff if their kids just think it.

And then in camp on Monday I will Get It.

I have to try to remember where my mittens spend July.

~~~~~~~

July 17, Saturday

Mom said, "You do not need mittens, Justin, it is July, and you can clean up your room if you have nothing to do."

That got me off the topic of mittens. I kept my hands in my pockets as much as possible the whole time after camp when I was hanging around in the kitchen with Mom instead of cleaning up my room, but then I forgot and left them on the table while we ate dinner out on the deck.

What Mom noticed: Elizabeth feeding most of her hot dog to Qwerty.

What Dad noticed: Qwerty throwing up the hot dog on the deck and then knocking over the lettuce plants when he tried to hide behind them.

What Qwerty noticed: that he is 100 times bigger than the lettuce plants. (Or maybe he didn't fully notice that, because he kept hiding there anyway.)

What Elizabeth noticed: the buns catching fire on the grill.

What I noticed: A person's red damaged knuckles are not so noticeable as you would expect to other people.

~~~~~~

July 18, Sunday

My best friend, Daisy, and her family came over for dinner tonight.

I straighten up my room for any friend coming over, not just Daisy. I don't care what Elizabeth says.

But it didn't matter anyway. Daisy didn't see if my room was straightened or a disaster.

For the first time I am happy I am not at Art Camp. I don't care if I have to swim 27 miles this summer and get my knuckles knocked clear off my fingers and wear horrible flip-flops because Dad and his toolbox repaired them instead of Mom and her credit card buying me new ones.

Daisy is supposed to be MY best friend. Not Elizabeth's. Elizabeth is supposed to be Destructo Baby and drive me and Daisy crazy while we are making up a show.

And Daisy's big grumbly brother Wyatt is supposed to just sit on the couch with his hair hanging over his eyes as he presses buttons on his phone.

Daisy is not supposed to spend her time before dinner in Elizabeth's room, trying out her pastels, even if they do both go to doofy Art Camp.

The only one you can count on in that family for doing what is expected is Wyatt.

I said, "How's camp, Daisy?"

She said, "Good."

I nodded for a while until finally she stopped smudging

clouds into the sky on her paper and asked, "How's your camp?"

I had a good answer of "So far, so good" all planned out and ready to go, but what came out of my mouth sounded a lot like "So far, no good."

She looked at me with sad eyes like I was a camp failure, so I went quickly to my room and closed the door until we got told to wash for dinner.

After dinner nobody came to look at my new collection of knights that I was playing with loudly with my door open just in case anybody was interested in joining in with that fun. Maybe it's because so far I have only five. Maybe five is not a very impressive strike force of knights. But still, they have powerful weapons, and there's also a dragon with fire painted many colors coming out of its mouth if people are so interested in paint.

These knights could attack if they came to life. They would attack people who bother me. They'd protect me. That is why they are all set up with their weapons pointed out my door at night, instead of at me in my bed—just in case any bad guys or bad girls come over to my house for dinner or anything and try to get into my room, which I do not want them to get into even if they wanted to come in.

It's not just because if the knights face me when I am trying to go to sleep in my bed for goodness' sake it freaks me out.

Elizabeth is not even in the grades yet. She doesn't know everything.

∿∿∿∿∿

July 19, Monday

Olympics training week is this week. I have to find a way to get out of going to this horrible camp. I can't do it, and I am falling into a million pieces.

Cash was the winner of Obstacle Course. He won a gold medal.

Second place, silver, was Montana C., and the bronze medal went to a kid named Koji. He does not speak a whole lot of English because his family normally lives in Japan, except for this summer. But you don't have to know English or any math facts or how to do any video games, which I am good at, or be a nice kid like Mom says I am to do Obstacle Course.

All you have to do is not let go of the metal bars and not fall in the mud.

Those are two of the skills I apparently do not have. Add them to the list.

Mud makes a sucking sound every time you fall in it, like it might pull you in and never let you out again.

On the bus ride home, I sat alone to think of what to say to Mom and Dad that would make them let me switch back to Science Camp and not be disappointed too much in me.

But then Montana C. plopped down next to me so I

couldn't think of a plan or even just be alone. We didn't talk to each other until she asked what was in my hand, and I said nothing.

I thought, *Well that was a great conversation. Maybe I could win the gold medal in having conversations.*

A few minutes later, she said she would trade me her silver medal if she could see what I held in my hand. I didn't want her medal (well I did but not as a trade), but her voice was getting loud, and it would be bad for people to hear a girl talking to me. Also I was tired.

So I opened my hand and let her see my shell.

"Wow," she said.

"Shhhh," I said.

"That is the most perfect-looking shell I've ever seen," she whispered.

That is why I let her hold it. Because she knew on first sight that it was perfect. She held it gently and looked at all the sides of it, then gave it back.

"It's my good-luck charm," I whispered.

She nodded and took off her silver medal.

"No thanks," I said.

"A deal's a deal," she argued.

"You won it," I said.

"Still."

I shook my head and looked out the window, holding my shell. If the only way I can ever get a silver medal is for somebody to owe it to me because I showed her my shell, forget it.

I didn't even say good-bye to Montana C. when I got off the bus, just "Excuse me" to get past her. Maybe that is rude, but we can't all be medal winners in life, even in manners competitions.

And that, I thought, was the end of that.

〰〰〰〰

July 20, Tuesday

Wrong.

"Justin!" Mom yelled from down in the basement last night, so I knew I was in trouble.

I just didn't realize how much.

I walked down the stairs to the main floor wondering what I had done wrong, then spent a few minutes looking at my knights, which I had left on the living room floor, thinking maybe Mom would forget about putting me in trouble if I didn't go down to the basement, until she called my name again.

So I went down to the basement to see what I had done wrong.

Mom was in front of the washing machine, with my wet suits dripping out of the washer, my wet towel on the floor, and Montana C.'s silver medal hanging on its red-white-and-blue ribbon from Mom's hand. Montana C. must have slipped it into my backpack when I wasn't looking.

"What is this for, Justin?"

I swallowed hard and thought about how to answer. "It is for coming in second in Obstacle Course in camp," I said.

Mom hugged me.

She told me how proud she was of me.

"No," I said. "It's not . . ."

"It's not gold?" Mom interrupted. "Oh, Justin, you don't have to come in first in everything! Silver is fantastic!"

At dinner, she and Dad both said I sure had made them proud and surprised them and that I was growing up so nicely.

"I know why you're surprised," I said to my salad. "Because you thought I was a loser."

"Justin!" said Dad.

"We don't use that word, Justin," Mom said. "And anyway it's not true."

"Yes, it is," I mumbled.

"We just thought you were more of a . . ." Dad said, and couldn't think of a word besides *loser,* so he looked at Mom. I looked at her, too.

"More of a sweetie," she said.

So in our family that is what we call a loser, I guess. A sweetie. It's almost worse.

When I went to bed last night, Montana C.'s medal was hanging from the post of the top bunk, staring at me like an all-knowing Cyclops. And all my stuffties stayed at the foot of my bed, turned away from the boy who did not admit the truth.

I stayed away from Montana C. all day today because now I can never return the silver medal she won and then slipped into my camp bag. I guess because she thought that was the only way I could ever get a medal.

I guess she thought I was a sweetie, too.

Maybe the one Olympics Training thing I am finally getting good at is hating girls.

~~~~~~

July 21, Wednesday

Relay Races is Camp GoldenBrook for *you thought you were swimming a lot before? Hahahahahaha.*

Relay Races means the same as it means in school, except at camp there's the twist of the relay races being in the pool.

While Mike the swim counselor was explaining about Relay Races, I was not paying attention because I was busy thinking about how to get out of relay races, like, maybe by a sore throat or broken arm, and also about what Cash had said.

Cash thinks maybe the space between my big toe and my second toe is so large because when I was born, I had six toes on each foot and one was amputated and my parents just never told me because they didn't want to scar me for life. And that would explain why I hate the horrible flip-flops of doom so much—because there is soreness where my extra toes aren't.

I was busy thinking about whether that might be true, and that is the reason I didn't know why Mike was calling my name. Instead of standing up and saying YES! like I should have, I sat there confused and said, "What?" which was funny, apparently.

It turns out Mike was calling my name because he wanted me to be Captain for one of the Relay Teams.

If you are Captain, you choose which kids you want on your team. While you stand in front, thinking about who is good and who is bad and how much you like or no thank you them, the other kids sit pulling up hunks of grass and pretending they don't really care if you pick them or if they are still sitting there still picking grass when most kids are already lined up behind somebody.

When you are Captain, nobody has a chance to either cheer or groan when your name is yelled out.

When you are Captain, you can't be one of the kids still pulling up hunks of grass trying to look like you aren't wishing to die because it is just you and Bartholomew Wiggins and Penelope Ann Murphy left sitting, and if you get chosen after

Bartholomew Wiggins or Penelope Ann Murphy, you might actually cry in camp.

When you are Captain, you get to stand up in front of all the other kids (except the other three Captains) and think to yourself, which of these kids do I want?

It is half great and half terrible, having that kind of power.

∿∿∿∿∿

July 22, Thursday

Dad said I never got any toes amputated don't be ridiculous.

Cash said, "Of course he would say that, he's your dad. He doesn't want you to feel bad. You think Pudding's dad tells her she's a loser?"

That made Xavier and Gianni laugh, but not me so much. I guess I was thinking about my feet. I never realized how strange my feet were before this, with the huge empty-toe space. But I have to wear the horrible flip-flops of doom down to swim anyway, despite my possible postamputation problems.

Also in my family, we don't use the word *loser*, so I am not allowed to answer about whether Pudding's father calls her a . . . thing that I am not allowed to say.

Probably if my parents knew a kid was being called Pudding in a not nice way, I would find out there is a rule against saying the word *pudding,* too, and then what would happen when my grandmother makes her special dessert? Would we say, *Wow, Gingy this is delicious . . . goo?*

So that is another reason why I can never tell my parents that kids are calling Penelope Ann Murphy the name of Pudding and that it's my fault. Because I don't think that would be fair to Gingy.

Actually, there might already be that rule in my family. Mom has a lot of rules I am not aware of ahead of time.

Though if Cash had said, *You think Pudding's dad tells her she's a sweetie,* I would not have known how to answer that either. Maybe he does call her a sweetie. Other people's parents can be completely unpredictable.

Because of my sore feet and

general slowness and lack of wanting to get down to the pool, I walked with Bartholomew Wiggins. He is in Shallow, too. But Bartholomew Wiggins doesn't even care that he is the worst Hawk except for Penelope Ann Murphy.

I don't know how he does that, how he can smile like he is listening to a happy song even when he misses the ball that came right at him and makes us lose, and then Cash and Xavier and Gianni (and in the background Koji and me, but we don't say anything just stand there with our arms crossed) all get mad at him because our archenemies, the Ravens, won at softball again.

The Ravens are only going into third grade, not fourth like us. They are practically in diapers, and they beat us, all because of Bartholomew Wiggins and his butterfingers.

While we played Knuckles I kept thinking *butterfingers butterfingers* and imagining if my fingers were made out of butter what would happen to them on a hot day like today.

Me and Koji and Cash and Xavier and Gianni are the ones who play Knuckles every day now. Girls and kids like Bartholomew Wiggins are not invited to play. We are the cool kids.

Being a cool kid kind of gives me a stomachache, but it is better than if people groan when they hear your name. I am the worst at sports of all the cool kids, so it is a very risky thing. Today Cash told Gianni to get out.

"*Get out!*" Cash yelled. It was with a quiet volume, but it sounded loud like trumpets anyway. Like fire alarms. Even though he said it with a quieter-than-indoor voice.

It was because Gianni said he didn't lose a round of Knuckles when he actually did. Gianni always cheats. He hates to lose is why. We go to school with him, but Cash just moved here from Tennessee, so he's not used to Gianni Schicci and his cheating ways. Last year, I used to wish somebody would say *Gianni Schicci, you are cheating and that is not allowed or you are out of the game.*

Well, today somebody did.

Gianni kicked rocks the rest of the day and squinted his eyes away from everybody. But it did not make me as happy that he finally got in trouble for cheating as I thought it would.

What it made me feel instead of happy was that I could get kicked out of being a cool kid very easily, too. So I have to just hold tight to my perfect shell and keep quiet and pretend I get the rules and also that it doesn't hurt when I get hit with the cards in Knuckles.

This is more like Acting Camp than even Sports Camp.

Unlike Bartholomew Wiggins and Gianni Schicci and me, Penelope Ann Murphy cries at what happens to her. A lot. Today after nobody wanted her as a tennis partner, she cried so hard her nose bled.

~~~~~~

July 23, Friday

Some kids did Swim a Mile today. You have to be in Blue to try for it. If you finish the Swim a Mile, you get a silver swim cap and you rule camp.

Gianni Schicci is in Yellow. He swam underwater when he was supposed to be doing freestyle and had to get out and be yelled at by James/Jay.

After our lesson finished, we were not allowed to just

relax. We had to go pick up the pennies that the counselors had sprinkled into the pool. I don't know how people get down that deep—all the way down to the way bottom of the pool—but in my opinion, the counselors should not throw their money away like that anyway. Another thing I don't know is if it's their own money, or the camp supplies the pennies. I kept popping up with empty hands and lungs. I was the only kid besides Bartholomew Wiggins to be floating moneyless and giving up again. The lifeguards blew their whistles and pointed to me and Bartholomew Wiggins and then at the side of the pool. The lifeguards don't talk. They just wear sunglasses and blow whistles. Sometimes they point. The regular counselors

and the swim counselors tell us what the different whistle sounds mean. This one meant that Bartholomew Wiggins and I had to keep our feet in, but we were allowed to wrap our towels around us. We just sat there with cold wet feet and dry hot heads.

"You still best friends with Noah?" he asked me after a while.

I shrugged. Noah is my second-best friend, but my best friend Daisy and I don't really play together or talk to each other anymore, so maybe Noah moved up a slot when I wasn't paying attention.

I was going to ask Bartholomew who he's best friends with, but then I thought what if he doesn't have any friends? Then he'd feel terrible. Or what if he wants to be my best friend? Then maybe I would have to say okay to that.

So I just splashed him with my foot instead of talking.

At arts and crafts, I made a bracelet for my mother for her birthday, which is this Sunday. Now that I'm going into fourth grade, I tend to think ahead more. Probably Elizabeth isn't making her anything.

It is made out of a lanyard with barrel stitch, which is

harder to do than the regular stitch. Bartholomew Wiggins is very good at barrel stitch, so he helped me. That was nice of him, especially when I hadn't picked him for my relay team or asked him who his best friend is or included him in Knuckles.

Though maybe that last thing was more kind than mean.

~~~~~~

July 24, Saturday

Tonight I am having a sleepover at Noah's house.

When I was younger, I was not allowed to go on sleepovers, but apparently I am old enough now. Xavier Schwartz and Gianni Schicci have them all the time. But I am not a big fan of sleepovers. I've had sleepovers of course but that was at my cousins' or grandparents' houses, and my parents were usually there with me. This would be without anybody who is normally in charge of me.

Other people's houses smell different, which is okay during the day but maybe not so good at night. Then when you are supposed to be sleeping, you can't, and you aren't playing anyway so really there is not a great reason not to be home safe in your own bed.

Also those noises could be bad guys.

And my stuffties would all be in my bed wondering, *Where is Justin? Where is he? When is he ever coming to bed? How can we sleep without Justin here with us?* They get very worried when I am not with them. They act all tough, but really they are small and soft and a little bit high-strung. And I would not be there. The whole night. When I am away for the night, my stuffties feel very unsturdy.

But most people do not understand about stressed-out stuffties, especially after their person already graduated from third grade.

Mom called Noah's mom to discuss privately her opinion that it would be a little hard for me to fall asleep over there without some of my stuffties, even though I am going into fourth grade and not a worried kid anymore.

"Oh, no problem," Noah's mom told my mom. "Noah sleeps with a bat."

So now what I am worried about is *Noah sleeps with a bat.*

I have seen Noah swing a bat—it is dangerous even if you are wearing a helmet and standing way across the diamond from him, like, at short center field. Just ask Robbie Cantrello.

You could get hit in the stomach by Noah's flying bat when he swings.

Noah may be my second-best friend, but the boy does not have a firm grip.

Also, why does Noah sleep with a bat?

And another worry I have now is maybe Noah's house is in a Bad Neighborhood is why.

~~~~~~~~

July 25, Sunday

It is a bat *stuffty* that Noah sleeps with. A bat that is like a mouse with wings, not like a wood stick to miss hitting a baseball with—a soft stuffty bat with sweet eyes and a small bashful smile. So even if Noah did for some reason swing it, that bat would not have hurt me too much.

He didn't swing it at all. He just secretly hugged it when he thought I wasn't seeing him.

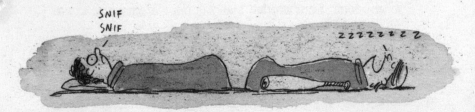

But his house is very cold in the night.

So I might have developed a cold and won't be able to participate in camp this coming week.

Especially in either Obstacle Course or in the Horrible Game whose name I am trying not to even think because of the risk I might say the word *knuckles* out loud if I think it too much or look up injuries to them on the Internet again.

As we ate pancakes for breakfast, Noah asked me, "How is Camp GoldenBrook?"

"So far, so good," I said. "How's Science Camp?"

He said it is awesome.

They are studying zoology this year, so they have an ant farm and fish and three lizards, two bunnies, and twenty eggs that might start hatching soon. He said the only bad thing about Science Camp is that I am not there with him.

Then we cleared our plates and played some games on his computer.

When Mom picked me up, I mentioned that maybe I should switch to Science Camp for the rest of the summer. She smiled in a slanted way and said she was happy I had had a good time with Noah but that they had already paid for the whole summer at Camp GoldenBrook and anyway I am doing so well there, don't be silly.

I buckled my seat belt and didn't be silly the rest of the way home.

We went to Mom's favorite restaurant for her birthday dinner. It has flowers on the table and also two candles, and even though the cups of coffee are very small, it takes Mom and Dad about an hour to drink them. But I didn't complain, because it was Mom's birthday. Only Elizabeth complained and then hid under the table pretending to be a cat while we waited for the check.

She didn't come out until it was time for Mom to open her gifts.

Mom liked her lanyard bracelet, even though it didn't fit around her wrist.

She said it would make a perfect key ring, which she has been needing a new one of.

Elizabeth made her a coffee mug at Art Camp. Mom said she has been needing a new coffee mug, too.

Either we are very smart kids or Mom needs a lot of new stuff.

∿∿∿∿

July 26, Monday

James/Jay made me do two laps around the soccer field in the middle of the game. I don't know why I was in trouble. I was just standing there, minding my own business, thinking about if anything rhymes with the word *pudding,* which is now what all the Hawks call Penelope Ann Murphy.

Which actually is my fault.

But I wasn't calling her that. I was just standing there, not thinking of a rhyme, watching clouds, maybe mumbling things like *gooding* and *shoulding.* And suddenly there was James/Jay, screaming my name right into my face with his stinky tuna breath saying, "Give Me Two Laps!"

It took me a minute to figure out that he meant I should run around the field twice, instead of give him two of something I did not even own. My first thought was that maybe *laps* is something like pancakes, and he wanted me to give him two of them.

I don't even know why I was in such big trouble. I think he just hates me.

‿‿‿‿‿

July 27, Tuesday

During breakfast, Elizabeth told us that her friend Eureka at Art Camp hated papier-mâché so much she asked to be excused from it yesterday. But at Art Camp, apparently, papier-mâché is a Must Do. So what Elizabeth's friend Eureka did was she put both her hands into the papier-mâché goo, turned a funny color, and then she threw up. All in the papier-mâché goo, all over her project and the art table and a little on the art teacher.

She got sent home, and from now on Eureka is excused from papier-mâché.

Eureka is Elizabeth's hero now.

"I thought you loved papier-mâché," Mom said.

"I do," Elizabeth said. "But now I know what to do if I don't like something."

And that is how I got my plan of how to get out of playing the awful game of Knuckles.

The only problem was it turns out I have about as much skills at throwing up when I want to as I do at hurdles or touching the bottom of the pool or swinging like a monkey on the rings. Which equals zero. Zero skills at any of those activities.

The best I could do at making myself puke was a burping/ grunting sound. By coincidence, it is the same sound I make when I do rings or hurdles. So maybe my special talent has finally been discovered.

Hideous noises. By Justin.

Hooray for me.

~~~~~~

July 28, Wednesday

I won at Knuckles.

That was the good news of the day. Also the big surprise. Because I still do not get how you play the game of Knuckles. I thought you just put down your pairs and then Cash says, "I win!" and you get hit with the side of the deck of cards.

But that did not happen today.

Today I put down my pairs, and then Cash said, "Hey, Justin won!"

And I had to hit him and Xavier and Gianni and Koji with the side of the deck of cards.

Everybody counts up the hits while the winner pounds

away. Xavier and Cash got one hit, and Koji got two. Gianni had to get hit seven times.

On the sixth hit, a little sound happened in Gianni's mouth halfway between "Ow" and crying.

And I still had to hit him one more time on those sore knuckles of his, which were red and maybe even had a drop of blood.

I hit him as light as I could, but Cash said, "No, you have to really give him a smack or it doesn't count."

So then I had to hit him again, an extra hit.

That was the bad news of the day.

The worst news of the day, though, was I knew I could never play Knuckles again.

Which meant I was going to have to do what I couldn't do: Tell.

∿∿∿∿∿

July 29, Thursday

All night last night, I had the word KNUCKLES in my mouth. I was daring myself to say it and daring myself to not say it. Then they made me take a shower when I wasn't even that dirty so I had to fuss about that and then take the shower and then I think the shampoo didn't get all the way out of my hair and then I had to play with my knights for a while and then it was time for Mom and Dad to say good NIGHT Justin fifty times even though I had an important thing to tell them but they said we can talk about it at breakfast.

I thought I would never fall asleep, but I guess I did because it seemed like ten minutes after they were saying good NIGHT Justin go to sleep stay in bed, they were saying good MORNING Justin wake up get out of bed.

I finally got up and brushed my teeth and went downstairs to breakfast, and while I was staring at my Toast-R-Cakes and my banana, I thought about telling them that I could not go back to camp because it was a horrible camp where they make you swing from rings even though you are not a monkey, and when the counselors are not looking, you have to play a horrible game called Knuckles.

But Elizabeth had a huge panic because she couldn't find the barrettes that she needed to wear, so I couldn't tell anything.

"I need them!" she kept shrieking.

"You don't need them," I told her. "You want them."

"No, I need them!"

"Elizabeth!" I yelled. "In life you need only food, water, shelter, and occasionally an umbrella. Everything else is a want."

Elizabeth, Mom, and Dad just stared at me. Nobody argued. Then my bus beeped, so I went off to torture camp.

Luckily today instead of Rest and the secret horrible game of Knuckles after lunch, we had to work on our Obstacle Course skills. Because we all stink. Especially me and Penelope Ann Murphy and Bartholomew Wiggins.

I didn't even mind, that's how much I hate Knuckles.

~~~~~

July 30, Friday

I sat at breakfast not telling. But then, after I cleared my bowl, I accidentally started telling.

Dad interrupted by saying, "Knuckles?"

"Yes," I answered.

"You're playing Knuckles at camp?"

I nodded my ashamed head.

"What's Knuckles?" Mom asked.

"I played it at camp, too!" Dad said. He laughed two ha's. "It's totally brutal, am I right, Justin?"

"Yes," I said.

"Justin?" Mom asked. "What's wrong?" She stopped sponging the counter and stared at me and Dad.

"It's a great game," Dad said. "Right, Justin?"

"No," I said. "It's a terrible game. And I am not allowed to tell about it, but I have to tell you because you said it's a rule I am not allowed to let anybody hurt me and they do hurt me! And I am not allowed to hurt anybody, but I do! I did! I hit Gianni Schicci with cards because I won, and . . ."

"You won?" Dad asked.

"Yes," I said. "Yesterday."

"Congratulations," Elizabeth said, and slurped the milk from her cereal bowl.

"Awesome, Champ," Dad said. "What hand did you play?"

"I don't know!" I said. "I don't even know how to play! And I hate it!"

"How can you win a game you don't even know how to play?" Elizabeth asked.

"I don't know!" I yelled.

"Would you please let him finish?" Mom yelled.

Qwerty sat down next to me and whined. I guess he figured he was in trouble, too. Elizabeth kept slurping her cereal and meowing, watching us all.

I didn't finish, though. Instead, I accidentally cried.

Mom hugged my head. I might have drooled a little on her sleeve. Either she didn't notice or mind. She told Elizabeth to stop purring go get her camp bag, and she kept hugging my head while I burped out the details in no particular order of the game of Knuckles and maybe also some about the rings and hurdles and that I am not a swim champ at all.

"Where are the counselors while you are playing this?" Mom asked.

"I don't know," I told her. "It's during snack. They're, I guess, eating."

"It's no big deal," Dad said. "It's a camp game."

"Look at his knuckles," Mom said.

"They'll heal," Dad said, and he passed his rough thumb gently over my bruised knuckles. "They'll be okay, Justin."

"What kind of supervision is this?" Mom asked. "Is this what we're paying all this money for? For our baby to be beaten up by a bunch of bullies with no adults taking notice?"

"Hey," Dad said. "If you don't like playing, Justin, play something else."

"I can't," I whispered.

"Yes, you can," Dad said back. "Be bold . . ."

"That's just a dumb poem," I mumbled.

"I'm calling your counselor, this morning," Mom said. "This game is not okay."

"You can't," I said. "Everybody will know I told."

"I'll tell them it has to be anonymous," Mom said.

"Ooo!" Elizabeth yelled, jumping twirling around the deck. "Anonymous is my favorite poet!"

That's when my bus beeped.

"I can't go to camp without a plan!" I shrieked.

Mom sent Dad out to tell the bus to leave without me. He

tried to argue, but it is not possible to argue with Mom when her face looks like *do not argue with me.*

I sank down into my chair and rested my damp face in my hands, listening to the bus pull away from my house without me. "I need a plan," I said.

"No, Justin," Elizabeth said, patting my arm. "All you *need* is food, water, shelter, and especially an umbrella. Everything else is a want."

∿∿∿∿∿

July 31, Saturday

Mom keeps asking if I want to talk about it. The answer keeps being no.

Because I do not want to talk about it.

I want to forget what Natalia told my mom when she called camp yesterday to complain about the horrible game of

Knuckles. Natalia, who I had been thinking might be the girl I was going to marry, told my mom that I was a, well, she did not use the word *sweetie*. Or *loser*.

The word she used was *maybe not having such a great summer at Camp GoldenBrook.*

She said she would sure keep a much closer eye on everybody at snack, and she was so glad my mom had called to let her know, especially because she has been concerned about me.

She told my mom the words *pretending to be hurt so he doesn't have to participate.*

And also the words *often close to tears* and the words *maybe not able to keep up physically.*

And when Mom said, "But he won the silver medal at Obstacle Course," Natalie used the horrible, horrible words, *I think you are mistaken.*

∧∧∧∧∧

Sunday, August 1

I am going to Science Camp.

It is where I belong.

I don't ever have to go back to Camp GoldenBrook. I never have to deal with Cash again, or James/Jay, or the impossible rings that my fingers cannot grip, or the swimming pool the size of an ocean with pennies down in the unreachable depths.

My parents are rescuing me from all that.

I never even have to face it again.

There is no shame in switching camps, Mom said. She and Dad are proud of me for trying something new. Not every new thing works out. They didn't think this was the right kind of camp for me from the beginning. This camp is kind of rough and tumble, and I am not such a rough-and-tumble kid.

And that is okay. That is not called being a failure.

I just should have told them it was awful and hard for me earlier, Dad said.

And then Mom gave me a kiss on my forehead and said, "Good night, sweetie."

So now I am lying on my bottom bunk with all my nice soft stuffties, not looking at my empty, crumpled Camp GoldenBrook backpack that I do not have to carry tomorrow, with Mom's kiss still on my forehead and the word *sweetie* smogging up my bedroom air.

And my oldest, best stuffty, Wingnut, looking sadly into my eyes.

~~~~~~~

August 2, Monday

I waited until the light coming through my window was enough to see Wingnut's smile. He knew what I had decided. I didn't even have to say it out loud to him. That's how well he knows me.

Then I tiptoed to Mom and Dad's room.

"Mom? Mom. Mom? Where are my swimsuits?"

"Shhh," she said. "Justin. Shh. Go back to bed. You aren't going back to Camp GoldenBrook, remember? Dad will tell the bus to go without you."

"We'll call Science Camp this morning," Dad said. "For today, you can, mmm, come with us to the store. Mmm." He rolled over and looked at his clock with one eye only. "It's five A.M., sweetie. What are you doing up?"

"I'm going back to Camp GoldenBrook," I said.

Their eyes opened. All four of their eyes looked at me, round and serious.

I took a big breath and smiled.

"I have to give it a shot," I said. "I have to be bold. Mighty forces will come to my aid. Don't worry."

Then I went down to the basement to find some swimsuits.

By the time the rest of the family came down to the kitchen, I was finishing my bowl of cereal.

"Justin, you don't have to . . ." Dad started, but I interrupted him.

"Yeah," I said. "I do."

"Okay," he said.

I went to sit out on the front step with my camp bag to wait for the bus.

At Free Play, time for Knuckles, Cash said, "You coming, Justin?" He flicked the top of his head toward the slide and waited, but I didn't say yeah.

The *yeah* in my mouth tried to get out, but I bit my teeth down hard and didn't let it.

"No thanks," I said, and sat down next to Bartholomew Wiggins, across the Parcheesi board from Marcus Snoot-Slutsky.

My heart was so pounding, but it was not just that I was not allowed to play the horrible game of Knuckles anymore that kept me there on the bench. It was also not just that Natalia kept winking at me and smiling encouragingly and staying close to me. It was also the idea in my head that if I was going to be brave at Camp GoldenBrook, I was going to have to be all the way brave. Even if my heart bursted right

out of my ribs onto Bartholomew Wiggins's Parcheesi set and
ruined it with goo and blood.

~~~~~~~

August 3, Tuesday

At Free Play today, Xavier Schwartz, who was right next to
Cash, said, "Hey, Justin Case, you playing today?"

"I'm bored of that game," I said.

Xavier and Gianni and Cash and Koji all stared at me like
I had said I hate candy or I love girls.

"Bored?" Cash asked.

"I mean, cards," I said. "No offense."

Cash's cheeks pinked up a little. "No," he said, and his
voice squeaked a little. He tried again. "I don't care." It still
squeaked a tiny bit. Cash is a new friend who will probably
never be an old friend, but still, he is hard to not like, despite
my best efforts all day.

"Let's play Bang Bang instead," I suggested.

"Yeah!" Gianni shouted.

"What's Bang Bang?" Xavier asked.

"It's a game me and Justin Case invented," Gianni
explained. Which was very weird because we hadn't. I hadn't

even invented it myself, really. I just made up the name of it on the spot.

"How do you play?" Cash asked.

"Well," I said. "You, just, you, what you do is, you make your hand into a gun . . ."

"And shoot each other!" Gianni yelled. "And you have to say, *'Bang bang!'* "

"And when you get shot you have to die," I said. "Until you count five Mississippis. Then you come back to life."

"Awesome," Xavier said.

"*Bang bang!*" Cash said, and I died a very twitchy, flopping death and stayed down on the grass for five wonderful and not-at-all-painful Mississippis before I got up and chased everybody.

~~~~~~~

August 4, Wednesday

I signed up for the swim test for Friday. I walked right up to that clipboard and put my name on the list to try for Yellow. James/Jay muttered, "Seriously?"

I heard him. He is probably right that probably I will fail and still be in Shallow. I still haven't picked up a single penny from the pool bottom. But maybe I will squeak by.

Also that is not a nice thing of him to say.

So I turned around and asked him, "Did you say something? I couldn't hear you."

I surprised both of us by asking that. We stood there on the pool deck, me skinny and little, him big and scary, looking surprised at each other about what I said.

"No," he mumbled.

"Good," I said, and walked past him, hoping the shaking

of my whole entire body wasn't as obvious to him as it was to me.

"What are you still doing in this camp?" is what James/Jay asked my back. "I heard you were quitting."

I didn't answer him. I watched my feet in the horrible flip-flops of doom walking to the bench, where I took them off and draped my blue-and-white-striped towel over the back. I told myself the words *say nothing say nothing* the whole way into the pool.

I worked hard in second swim and didn't come as close to drowning as usual, even though I tied again for last place with Bartholomew Wiggins the first lap. But I did a second lap, so if it had been a contest for who can do more laps—me or Bartholomew Wiggins—I would've won.

Then I got a cramp and had to rest my shivering body. My toe meat was all shriveled up.

So luckily it wasn't a contest for who could stay in the pool the whole swim period—me or Bartholomew Wiggins—because that one I would've lost.

At Quad, Cash and Xavier and Gianni and Koji were laughing about something Cash was telling them. I sat on my

towel away from them and sang loud and clear all the words that I could remember of the song "Baby Shark."

Natalia crouched down beside me and asked, "You okay, Justin?"

Some crying wanted to start inside my eyes, but I breathed in through my nose and convinced my mouth to curve into a smile. Then I looked up into Natalia's brown eyes, and I said what I had been saving up for her:

"So far, so good."

~~~~~

August 5, Thursday

Bartholomew Wiggins was absent from camp today.

Which left me on the grass, last boy, just me and Penelope Ann Murphy, with Cash next to choose.

In Science Camp they don't choose teams, they do experiments.

He chose Penelope Ann Murphy.

I think it's because I said no to Knuckles, and now every Hawk loves Bang Bang best of all games. But right then it was baseball time, and Cash was pitching for his team. I was up last for my team. I kept striking out, every time. It is a long walk away from the plate when you strike out with Cash smiling at you. I did not want to do that walk again.

Cash pitched a slow, fat one right across the plate. I swung and watched the bat wallop that ball, smack across the red stitches.

It hit Cash hard—*boom!*—in the belly.

He made the sound of *oof*.

And people laughed.

So that was a tiny and very wonderful piece of revenge, even if it means I am a terrible person for feeling that way.

The *oof* of Cash when I hit him with a baseball in the belly is now ranked with my shell, gummy worms, and Nothing to Worry About in my top-five favorite things of life.

I have not yet decided what the fifth is. I am keeping that space open for something really excellent.

I am trying to think only of those top-favorite excellent things in the world instead of the swim test I have signed up to take tomorrow.

Because when I think of that swim test, it makes the chance of falling asleep tonight smaller and smaller and smaller.

~~~~~~

August 6, Friday

What I hate:

1. Tests, especially in summer.

2. Water up my nose.

3. The color red, which is for Shallow.

What I love:

1. My new swim cap.

2. Which is yellow.

3. Hearing, "Yay, Justin Case!" from Xavier Schwartz, even
   though he has a Blue cap, so probably he thinks Yellow

is not that great, but still he slapped me on the back so hard it felt like I might go flying back into the pool.

4. Not flying back into the pool because even though my body was so tired from the swim test it managed to stay exactly where it was.

~~~~~

August 7, Saturday

It was a hurricane today.

We had to stay inside and bake bread and then

chocolate-chip cookies all day. Dad put masking tape in Xs on all the windows while the bread dough started to rise. Then we took turns punching the dough. We pretended it was bad guys and we were heroes.

I pretended I was not scared at all of a hurricane ripping our house up and possibly tumbling us around like we were socks in the dryer. Mom and Dad and Elizabeth believed me, but there were a few stuffties on my bed who looked at me with *I don't think so, Mister* looks in their doubting plastic eyes.

The hurricane didn't quite brew itself into anything more than rain. It was kind of a dud of a hurricane.

But I got to lick the whole bowl plus both beaters while the cookies baked because Elizabeth was in trouble for sneak-eating so many chocolate chips. So it was a pretty cool day.

Especially each time I thought of the color yellow.

〜〜〜〜〜

August 8, Sunday

We went to the beach, just our little family. No other family, no grandparents. I thought it was going to be kind of boring, but it wasn't. We built a sand castle and stayed out for dinner at Dock's.

Elizabeth was drawing on the paper tablecloth. I wanted to also, but I was being grown-up and boring so I didn't. When tomato sauce dripped on her picture of a unicorn or maybe it was a fire truck, she shrieked and jolted back from the table, so a glop of tomato sauce tumbled onto her flip-flop.

I thought she might fall down on the floor screaming about that, but she didn't. She froze, staring at the glop.

"There's sauce on my flip-flop," she whispered.

"Here's a napkin," Dad offered.

She lifted her suddenly pale face up to look at him with eyes like brown M&M'S. "I think I have to go wait in the car."

She started walking slowly away from the table, her toes crunched up to avoid the sauce. Mom shrugged at me and Dad. We both smiled.

Mom placed her napkin on the table, stood up, and dashed quietly to Elizabeth. She put her arm around Elizabeth's narrow shoulders and, whispering, guided her to the ladies' room. Dad and I paid the check and went out on the deck of Dock's to wait for Mom and Elizabeth to finish coping with the sauce disaster.

The moon, fat and white, was heavy and low, melting into the water right across from us.

"Hey, Dad," I said.

"Mmm-hmm?"

"Let's swim to the moon."

"Okay," Dad said.

"Looks like we could do it," I said.

"Sure," he said, and put his heavy hand on my shoulder.

"Might take us five hours," I said.

"Mmm-hmm. But, if you want to, we can."

I leaned against him. He was big and solid as a tree.

"Yeah, Dad," I said. "Let's swim to the moon."

~~~~~~

August 9, Monday

Color War is going to happen in camp sometime in August but not yet so everybody is supposed to stop asking about it.

I wasn't. I had no questions about it until now.

I know what *color* means and I know what *war* means.

But the combination does not make any sense to me. Color War? How can that be a camp activity? Unless it has to do with paints in the arts-and-crafts cabin and some behavior I don't think the grown-ups in charge would (or at least should) allow.

But at Camp GoldenBrook, you never know.

Even though I don't know what a Color War exactly is, I can tell that it is something very exciting. I know that because when Miss Lisa announced that Color War will break out soon, who knows when, be alert for signs, everybody went nuts. It was like she was saying we all just won a million bucks each and a trip to Disneyland. Me and Bartholomew Wiggins and Koji were the only Hawks who were still just sitting on our towels.

We are the only Hawks who weren't Ravens last year.

Bartholomew Wiggins said he is a pacifist so maybe he won't have to do Color War.

I am not sure what a pacifist is, but I am thinking I might be one, too, because those kids had very wild looks in their eyes while they were shouting, "Color War! Color War!"

Except that I think a pacifist is the thing my baby cousin used to suck on, so maybe not. When he was a baby sucking a pacifist, my cousin was almost as drooly as my dog.

〜〜〜〜〜

August 10, Tuesday

In my opinion the word *pacifier* sounds a lot like the word *pacifist*.

In my other opinion, it is not nice for parents to laugh at their own son who is asking a question about vocabulary, which they should encourage him to expand.

Even if they say they are laughing with him. You can't laugh with a person who is not laughing.

I was not being overly sensitive.

If my knights came to life, they could seriously injure anybody who laughed at me or with me or fixed my horrible flip-flops of doom with something out of his toolbox called Duck Tape. I don't know if it's made of ducks or it's tape you hold ducks together with, but if I can't just get the kind of flip-flops Bartholomew Wiggins has, the kind without the pole between the big toe and other toes, my parents could at least tape my horrible flip-flops of doom with flip-flop tape. And also they could at least not keep saying they don't want to fight with me about it because they are pacifiers.

All I would have to do is order my knights to attack, and they would be so sorry.

~~~~~~

August 11, Wednesday

We thought it was Color War breaking out today, but no. It was just a garbage truck rumbling up to the mess hall.

I signed up to take the swim test again Friday. I have to get into Deep before this summer is allowed to end. I have to.

I don't care that James/Jay shook his head while I was writing my name on the clipboard sign-up sheet. But he did not have to say the words *just give it up.*

And when we did Obstacle Course, he did not have to say the words *oh, for Pete's sake.* I don't know who Pete is, but if I can't hang on to the rings or jump over the hurdles for my own sake, I don't see how Pete comes into it.

I don't think there even is a Pete. I think James/Jay was

just being mean again, in front of all the other campers, when he should have said some encouraging words like, *you can do it* or, even better, *that's okay, no problem, you can skip that section of the obstacle course, Justin.*

When I got home, I found Qwerty whining in the front hall. He was sad because Mom started taking him to Obedience School today. She told me, right in front of Qwerty, that he is the worst dog in the whole class.

Qwerty looked very ashamed about that.

I told Mom that Qwerty will probably get Most Improved Dog, or even become the best dog in the whole class by the end of the course, but she shook her head and kind of laughed and said, "Well that would be a big surprise."

So I took Qwerty out back to teach him some tricks, starting with the game of fetch.

Qwerty is very enthusiastic, but he still doesn't get the rules of that game, no matter how many times I explain them.

Mom might have a good point about his lack of potential, but maybe not. Some of us are just late bloomers. So I am not giving up on him yet. I will never give up on him. I am just taking a break to rest for a while.

~~~~~

August 12, Thursday

Too bad for Qwerty that there is not a dog named
Bartholomew Wiggins in his Dog Obedience class.

There is only one reason I am not the worst boy in the
whole Hawks group at lacrosse, and that reason is called
Bartholomew Wiggins.

On the other hand, I am pretty fast at running, especially
when it is in the game of tag and Gianni Schicci is chasing me
with something on his finger that definitely looks like it
recently came out of his nose.

Cash said if I am on his team in Color War, we will rock at
running races.

What I said to that was, of course, "Yeah."

I might have to pay Gianni Schicci to chase me with boogers.

⌇⌇⌇⌇⌇

August 13, Friday

It doesn't matter that I didn't make it into Deep. Mike said, "Great try, Justin. You are really improving." I almost said back his favorite word of *whatevs*, but I just shrugged instead. I was just giving it a shot. I didn't think I'd actually make it into Deep. I still haven't gotten even one cent off the pool bottom. Xavier is practically a millionaire.

James/Jay definitely didn't think I would make Deep, either. He didn't say anything this time. He turned his back to me while I was getting out of the pool. I heard him do a loud breathing out, because I guess he was out of breath from the effort of watching me not get into Deep.

What I thought of saying to him: *Shut up, you mean person.*

What I actually said: nothing.

What I will say to him someday: *Hahahahaha, I am in*

Deep now, and you are still a mean person. So only one of us improved this summer.

My best friend Daisy is afraid of Friday the Thirteenth.

I might call her on the phone later to see how she's doing, but probably not. It might be too weird, and I am pretty much too worn out from my life these days to try anything else that might make me feel lousy.

〰〰〰

August 14, Saturday

There were as many mosquitoes as berries at the Pick Your Own farm we went to today. And about twice as many gnats. We had to keep our mouths shut, or the gnats would just fly right down our throats, which meant we couldn't complain as much when the moms put their two favorite screens (bug and sun) on us.

Montana C. said without opening her lips that we should put on Little Kid Screen, too, to protect us from her little brother Buckey and my little sister Elizabeth.

So I sprayed her with pretend Little Kid Screen.

While I was doing it, I made a wish that it wouldn't seem

like I was the little kid myself, pretending to have a magic
spray.

My wish came true because she took the pretend (and
invisible) bug spray from my hand and sprayed me with it, too.

She smiled without opening her mouth at all but it was still nice.

We got the most berries of any team, including the parents'. Buckey and Elizabeth were the losing team by a lot. They had almost no berries in their bucket at all, but I think they ate most of what they picked. Which is called stealing. But they didn't get in trouble, even when Elizabeth said, "Come on, Buckey, let's go as far as we can!" and they ran to the last row.

Every time Montana C. and I opened our mouths to talk, we swallowed gnats. Then we both did a lot of spitting to get rid of the gnats in our mouths. She is excellent at spitting long distances. Just like she is excellent at everything, pretty much. She's in Deep, of course.

In the farm store, after the parents paid for the berries we'd picked, they also got us a bushel of peaches to share, since Elizabeth and Buckey were begging and pleading for them. The farm people had already picked the peaches so Montana C. and I didn't care, and also we are older so we don't beg.

We each got to eat one peach and save one for tomorrow because they are not cheap.

Peach juice dripped down my chin when I bit into my peach of today, but that was okay because the same thing was happening to everybody's chin. We all made slurping noises.

My new favorite foods in the world: raspberries and peaches.

My new least favorite food in the world: gnats.

My new second-favorite sound in the world: slurping.

My new favorite sound in the world: Montana C. cracking up when I told her my new least favorite food.

~~~~~~

August 15, Sunday

"A Sad Song About My Peach"

I feel sad about my peach

My little little peach

That I ate

It was good and it was ripe

But now it's down the pipe

My sweet little peach

That I ate

∿∿∿∿∿

August 16, Monday

Montana C. sat with me on the bus to camp this morning.

All day the boys in the Hawks said, "Oooooo, you love her. You want to marry her."

I said, "Shut up."

But I thought, *Well, maybe I do.*

And then the whole rest of the day, I kept thinking that thought. Well, sometimes I got distracted and thought about why would they throw pennies onto the floor of the pool because isn't that dangerous to the plumbing if they get sucked down the drain and how many cookies I would eat if I had infinity cookies or what would Mom do if I turned into a giraffe.

But then I got right back to the thought of maybe I will marry Montana C. when we grow up now that Natalia is definitely out.

∿∿∿∿∿

August 17, Tuesday

On the way to Newcomb, I mentioned to Xavier Schwartz that it would be really bad if we were two-dimensional because if a big wind or even a tiny wind came, we'd be blown right down.

"Okay," Xavier said.

Which made me think maybe that was a dumb thing to say. Maybe other people don't worry about if we were 2-D. Maybe worrying about that is proof that I am weird and not at all cool. And maybe even still a worried kid.

"You know what else would be bad?" Xavier asked.

What I thought was, *Saying a weird worry out loud when you should keep it to yourself?* but what I said instead of that was, "What?"

"If our internal organs were on the outside."

"Ew," I said. "Like ornaments on a Christmas tree?"

Xavier cracked up. "Yeah," he said. "Brain on top, like a star."

"Guts wrapped around the middle," I said.

"Like tinsel," Cash said, coming up on my other side.

"Yeah," Xavier and I said.

"Disgusting," Gianni said. "Think of the ooze."

"That really would be bad," I said. "Gut tinsel."

"It would be awesome!" Xavier shouted.

"If you got a little cut, you could sever a major artery," I said. "And plop, there would be your heart on the ground."

Just as I was thinking, *Whoops, did I say a weird thing again?* all three of them cracked up. I laughed, too. Maybe it was from relief a little bit but also from picturing guts and plopping hearts.

Then we got to the upper fields and saw there were balls all over the soccer pitch, organized into letter shapes.

The letters were *C-O-L-O-R W-A-R.*

Which means that Color War had broken out.

So we all had to shout our heads off and tackle each other.

〜〜〜〜〜

August 18, Wednesday

In Science Camp we sang songs like, "I want to walk (clap, clap) a mile in your shoes, to walk a mile in your shoes."

In Camp GoldenBrook during Color War we sing, "We are the Blue Team. Beat up the Red Team!"

It is not nice to threaten to beat up the other team just because they are the other team. Wanting to walk a mile in the other person's shoes is nice.

But singing, "Beat 'em up beat 'em up rah rah rah," is kind of a little bit fun. Maybe this camp is changing me into a rough-and-bad kid.

<center>~~~~~~</center>

August 19, Thursday

All day all we do is Color War. We have to beat the Red Team. We beat them at pick up pennies from the floor of the pool (I didn't get any), but they beat us in Newcomb and then at tennis round robin.

Cash and I were doubles partners. I was pretty good at getting out of his way when he was going for the ball. Better than Gianni was at getting out of Xavier's way, which is why Gianni got a racquet sandwich.

I offered to walk Gianni to the nurse. It would be fair that way—Xavier and Cash could play each other in singles.

James/Jay said no. "*Tough it out*," he said to Gianni. Then when Gianni really couldn't get his mouth into the right shape, he made Gianni walk it off down to the nurse by himself. It is true that even though his bottom teeth were all to the right of his top teeth, his legs were fine. But in school if you have to go to the nurse, somebody has to walk you.

I thought that was a general rule, or a law, in this country.

While Gianni went to the nurse to have his jaw put back in the right part of his face, Xavier got to partner up with Montana C. James/Jay yelled at me the word *focus* when the ball Montana C. served zoomed past my left ear. I was busy watching Gianni walking sadly and hunched down the hill. I didn't know we'd started again.

"Focus" is what Qwerty doesn't have at his obedience class. He gets in trouble, too. Maybe it runs in my family. I held my racquet with both hands and crouched over, but I didn't even see the ball that time, just heard it as it passed me. James/Jay made doglike grunting noises and searched the clouds to see if my focus was hovering up there, maybe. It wasn't.

But that behavior of his gave me one minute of an enemy other than the Red Team.

Xavier and Montana C. won. By a lot. Very quickly.

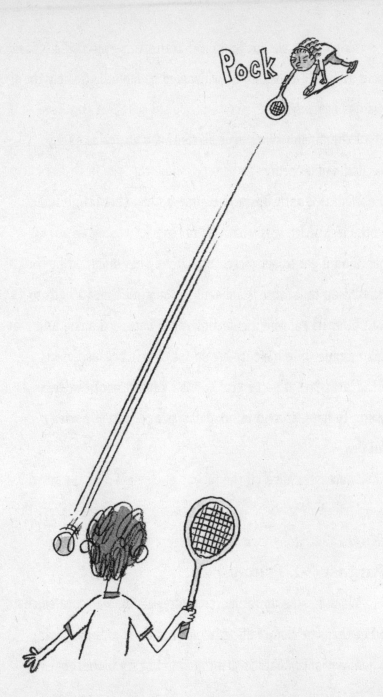

"Next week we are going to have to win everything," Cash said at Quad. And then he whispered to me very fiercely the words *get ready*.

I think Color War might be tied with Knuckles as my second-worst enemy.

Also tied with Obstacle Courses, swim tests, and lime popsicles, which was what was for snack.

Gianni got to get picked up early by his mom, so he missed all that stuff. Mom said it was a nice idea I had, to call him. He said he was feeling much better, thanks, and that his mom let him have ice cream for dinner because of his dislocated jaw. Also he gets to miss camp tomorrow. He is going to hang around in his pajamas and watch movies all day.

Some guys have all the luck.

~~~~~~

August 20, Friday

When I came up to my room after camp, I discovered that while I was at camp failing to get into Deep and not crying when James/Jay/Barf Breath rolled his nasty bloodshot eyes

about my lousiness at swimming, Qwerty had been busy
chewing up two of my new knights.

Elizabeth said maybe the knights were attacking Qwerty,
and he just had to defend himself.

That made me so mad, all my furious of the whole
built-up summer of mad came vomiting out of my mouth. I
yelled at her and at Qwerty, too, that that was the stupidest
thing ever, and I don't even care if we are not allowed to use
the word *stupid* or the word *hate* or to let anybody hurt us or
be quitters in our family. Because it is all so dumb and we all
know it! It doesn't even matter! Because of course the knights
were not attacking Qwerty! They are just stupid plastic toys!

I am not sure who looked at me most sadly after that, but it was not Elizabeth, who stomped away saying that I was in big trouble. It was a tie of sad faces between Qwerty and the one completely non-gobbled knight, the traitorous bad guy whose name is Steeltrap.

I think Qwerty's face looked sorrier but Steeltrap's face looked more betrayed. Not like he was winking his one closed eye in a cool *we share a secret* way but more like an *I can't bear to look at you with both my eyes* kind of way. Even though those gobbled knights are his sworn enemies, he has never betrayed them as badly as I just did.

The gobbled knights were in too much pain from being chewed up by a big drooly dog to look at me at all.

But I can't waste my time thinking about the feelings of knights or dogs. I have to spend my weekend getting ready for when Monday comes around. I am going to get a lot of sleep and eat a lot of healthy food and maybe do some push-ups or other toughening-up activities this weekend.

For now, I am going to sleep in the top bunk of my bed for sure the whole night tonight, no getting scared and moving down later like last time. It's not just to avoid Qwerty and his whining and his huge tongue. And it is not to avoid any vengeance the knights might try to mount during the night.

I meant it—nobody could be scared of them. They are just plastic toys, and their small weapons probably couldn't hurt me very much even if they did come to life. Which I don't believe in.

Very much.

The reason I have to sleep up top tonight is that the stuffties down in the bottom bunk are too complicated. Bananas, who is President of the Bed, and Snakey, who is not, are in a fight. Some of the other stuffties are whispering rumors that Snakey secretly likes Bananas, which he denies. And the leader of the Snakey Likes Bananas teasing is Rally, another rough stuffty who has been Snakey's best friend since he joined the bed.

It is a mess.

And if I don't get enough sleep, I am a mess, too.

That is why I am up here, so close to the ceiling, with just Wingnut, Baloney, Fleecebelly, and Squirt, who are all very calm stuffties. We are all trying not to think about how far we are right now from the floor and what a big week we have ahead of us. We are ignoring the creaking sound that probably does not mean that this bed really does need some screws tightened right away.

Maybe we should go ask Dad and his toolbox to check it out again. Because maybe last time he checked, there was a screw he forgot to check, or maybe one of the knights, for example possibly Steeltrap, secretly did come to life and used his weapon to loosen the screws to get back at me for what I said.

Even if Dad yells, "Go to SLEEP, Justin" again, maybe it would be worth getting him to just check for safety. Because if I have a bunk-bed crash, I am not going to be able to be the hero of Color War next week.

Which is my secret plan.

I am telling myself with every breath in that I am safe up here. Noah is not so brilliant—he once got seven wrong on a ten-word spelling test. I will not fall out of this very high top bunk and smash into a thousand bits no matter what Noah says.

With every breath out, I am telling myself, I will still be up here tomorrow morning when I wake up.

~~~~~~~

August 21, Saturday

When I woke up this morning, I was not on my top bunk.

I opened my eyes in the middle of a dream where I was being chased through the whole ocean by a big whale with horrible pointy gunky teeth. I was breathing hard, still thinking I was running through deep water away from an angry whale, but I wasn't. I had no idea where I was, though, other than NOT on my top bunk and not being eaten by a crazy whale.

I thought maybe I had fallen off and smashed into a thousand bits so I was dead.

I didn't feel dead, but I have never been dead before, so maybe I didn't know that this is how dead feels. I was not always alive, of course, but I don't remember the time before I was born. It was too long ago.

And I don't know if that would feel the same as dead feels anyway. I thought about being not yet alive and being dead for a while, and if that is the same or different. Also I wondered if I was one of those types of not-alive—the not-anymore version, specifically.

But then I decided that it would be weird to feel this alive and sweaty and in pajamas with a very annoying and itchy tag at the neck if I were dead. If I were dead, I probably would not feel so sparky.

Being dead seemed less likely the more I considered it. Especially because I could hear waves.

So then I thought, *Maybe global warming happened and the ocean swallowed up the land all the way to our backyard.*

But that wouldn't explain why I was lying in a top bunk bed that was not my top bunk bed. Global warming is powerful stuff, but still, I don't think it could sweep a kid from one top bunk bed onto another top bunk bed.

Anyway, it hadn't.

We were just at Gingy and Poopsie's beach condo. Dad carried/walked me out to the car after bedtime, and apparently we had a whole conversation about whales on the way.

I don't remember that at all, which is too bad because Dad said it was very interesting and also funny. He and Mom looked at each other and smiled about that. A lot of the time it is Elizabeth they look and smile at each other about, so I might have to do some whale research when we get home, to keep my streak going with them on that.

Later on, Dad handed me a piece of paper from Gingy's notepad. It had pictures of shells and starfish preprinted on it, and also Dad's writing. The writing was of that poem Dad liked by the poet with the girl's name of Gerta: "Be bold, and mighty forces will come to your aid." But this time under the poem was the name of Goethe.

I guess a lot of people had the idea of that poem.

I said thanks to Dad and tucked that piece of paper into my shorts pocket with my perfect shell. Then I changed into my swimsuit so I'd be ready for kids' swim time. I need the whole two hours. I have big plans in mind for the last week of camp.

~~~~~~

August 22, Sunday

Today it was thick-hot out, but the waves down at the beach were too rough so the red DO NOT GO IN THE WAVES, YOU NUMBSKULLS flag was up. We were swimming in the pool, where I was working more on my strokes because of the Color War relay races tomorrow and my big idea for dominating. All the adults were saying I must be the champion swimmer of camp and other nice stuff like that. It was not true, but it was very fun to pretend it was.

At exactly noon on the dot, Mr. Cranky Pants yelled, "Those kids have to get out of the pool."

Mom said, "Come on out, kids."

Elizabeth and I said, "Aww." But we were getting out. We were already swimming toward the ladder.

We are not the fastest swimmers in the world, is all, especially Elizabeth who goes to Art Camp.

Mr. Cranky Pants said, "They have to get out! It's the rule! They have to get out!"

"They are getting out," Gingy said calmly, still reading her magazine. "Relax. It's a hundred degrees. Don't stress yourself."

"There are rules!" Mr. Cranky Pants said, pointing at the sign, where about a thousand rules were listed in tiny print. "Kids are only allowed in the pool between ten and twelve! Rules!"

We climbed out. Mom wrapped Elizabeth in a towel. I sat down on my towel with my feet dipped in the deep end, the way we do on hot days at camp. The pool water completely evaporated off me in about one second.

"He can't have his feet in the pool," Mr. Cranky Pants yelled from the shallow end, where his big hairy belly was still above the water, floating on top. "There are rules!"

"His feet aren't bothering you," Gingy said, without looking up from her magazine. She likes to sit in the shade of an umbrella. Though she wears her fancy swimsuit with ruffles and bows under her fancy swimsuit dress, she does not care much for getting into the pool herself. Unlike Poopsie, who wears huge scuba goggles and does cannonballs.

"His feet ARE bothering me," Mr. Cranky Pants said. "I am entitled to do my laps without children's feet in the pool."

"Oh, for goodness' sake," Mom muttered. "Justin, take your feet out of the pool, please."

So I did.

I sat crisscross applesauce and watched Mr. Cranky Pants slowly dog-paddle toward the deep end. His slow head stayed above the water. His kicks barely broke the surface. When he got to about the halfway mark, he stood up and said, "I don't think children are even allowed to be in the pool area when it's past children's hours."

"It's a heat wave," Dad said kindly, kneeling down on the edge of the pool. "If they promise not to make even a ripple, do you think they could just dangle their feet in the water?"

"No!" Mr. Cranky Pants shook his head and his bouquet of

chins jiggled underneath. "There are rules! No children!" He splashed the water with his open palm. "No children! That's the rules!"

"Come on, kids," Mom said. She stood up.

Gingy stood up, too. "Rules my eye," Gingy said, taking off her hat, her sunglasses, and the ruffled dress she wears over her bathing suit. She slammed her magazine down on top of her pile of clothes and marched toward the shallow end. We all watched.

"Rules are rules," Mr. Cranky Pants muttered, a little less loudly, and started his slow dog paddle toward the deep end again, moving slowly but surely away from Gingy.

"Yes," Gingy said, stomping down the pool steps, splashing. "Rules are rules. And you wouldn't want my grandchildren's tiny feet interrupting your massive butterfly stroke. And you are entitled. Oooo, are you entitled."

"That's right," Mr. Cranky Pants practically whispered, quickening his little doggy-paddle strokes, a pucker of worry on his mouth.

By then Gingy was standing in the shallow end. She lurched forward and started kicking up a storm, heading straight toward Mr. Cranky Pants. "But I am not a child," Gingy shouted. "I am entitled to swim as much as I want right now."

Gingy swam past Mr. Cranky Pants, splashing him right in the face as she passed him. At the deep end, Gingy grabbed onto the edge and winked at me. "Justin, honey, would you please get your old grandmother that red kickboard? Thanks, love."

Gingy held on to that kickboard and practiced her kicking right exactly wherever Mr. Cranky Pants tried to swim.

His face kept getting splashed with a turbojet of water from Gingy's kicks.

We couldn't believe it. Gingy is the nicest person I have ever met. With the best manners.

Elizabeth's mouth was hanging open. So was Mom's and so was Dad's and mine was, too. Not Poopsie's, though. Poopsie was standing by the side of the pool with his arms crossed, smiling down at his wife in the pool.

Mr. Cranky Pants stood up. He walked the rest of the way across the shallow end and slowly yanked himself up the stairs, out of the pool.

As he wrapped his grumbling self in his towel, Gingy yelled out, "Does anybody mind if my grandchildren cool themselves off in the pool? Do I hear a motion to suspend the rules during a heat wave?"

"So moved," Poopsie yelled.

"Seconded," yelled Mom.

Mr. Cranky Pants banged the gate behind him as Gingy walked up the steps out of the pool toward her chair.

Before he challenged me and Elizabeth to a cannonball contest, Poopsie gave Gingy a kiss right on her mouth.

〰〰〰

August 23, Monday

I hate how Bartholomew Wiggins pokes me when he's talking to me and I hate how itchy my neck gets when sweat dries on it and I hate blisters and I hate that Penelope Ann

Murphy cries every time she comes in last in a thing, which is basically every time she does a thing.

But what I hate even more than any of that is tetherball and also the word *love*.

Especially after today.

As I waited in line behind her at the tetherball tournament, I could see that Penelope Ann Murphy was kind of vibrating, like a string on a guitar after the counselor strums it and it's still blurry and hummy.

I got closer to see if any sound would be humming out of her.

It wasn't.

But I noticed while I was close to her that, wow, she really, really smelled like pudding. Also that the fingers of her left hand were touching a ring she was wearing on her other hand. It had some sticky-uppy elements that were pretty cool.

So I said, "Hey, Penelope Ann."

She turned around with her red face right next to mine and yelled, "What now?"

Which made me take a step back and bump into Cash,

who was behind me. But I didn't fall down. I said, "I like your ring."

She squinted her eyes at me. "Are you teasing me?"

"No," I said.

"What, then?" she asked.

"It's fancy," I said. "I like the sticky-uppy elements. Also the, um, colors. Of it. The ring."

She smiled a tiny smile. "Thanks," she whispered. Then people were yelling at her to go, go—it was her turn, so she stepped forward onto the sand.

Gianni Schicci served the ball.

Penelope Ann Murphy ducked the first time the ball came whirring around, but then, as it came again, Penelope lifted her right hand and punched it—hard.

She connected with a ball in the right way for the first time of the entire summer. She hit that ball with such force, sparks flew from it.

Colored sparks.

Sparkly sparks.

They fluttered through the air like the grand finale of a fireworks show, and I opened my mouth to cheer, but no

sound came out because I realized that those were not sparks and they were not fireworks.

They were what used to be Penelope Ann Murphy's ring.

In slow motion, that ring just exploded into a million pieces that rained down all over the sand.

Gianni punched the ball back, and it wrapped the rope all the way around the pole. Another point for the Red Team.

They all cheered.

Penelope knelt down on the sand and gathered up the molecules of her shattered ring. I got down and picked up some ring bits, too. She grabbed them from my hand without even saying thank you.

Then she stood up, covered in sand and sweat. Her lower lip started to tremble. Her cheeks were jiggling like Jell-O, my least favorite food. Then her eyes overflowed, and she was crying and gulping air and drooling more than my dog Qwerty. It was about ten kinds of awful at once.

Behind me the Blue Team started mumbling and whispering the usual stuff: She is such a loser, and why'd she have to be on our team?

"You made us lose again, Pudding," Cash said, a little louder, and to her.

"Leave me alone!" Penelope screamed. Her palms were full of ring bits, so she had to wipe her nose with the back of her hand. "Just leave! Me! Alone!"

"Ew!" Cash said back. "You are so—"

"Stop, Cash," I said, before I thought it through.

"Why? Is Pudding your girlfriend?" Cash asked me, his face all scrunchy and mean. "You love her now, too?"

"No," I said.

"You do!" he said. "Did you give her that ring? You did! You're gonna marry her? You love her!"

"No," I said. "I'm not marrying anybody. I'm going into fourth grade. Duh."

Xavier giggled at that.

"I didn't give her the ring, obviously. But it's hers, and she liked it and it broke. You'd cry, if that happened to you, right, Xavier?"

"No."

"Your trophies?" I asked.

"Oh," he said. "Well, sure, if my trophies broke. But, I mean, they're trophies."

"I don't have any trophies," Penelope Ann Murphy said, not helping her cause at all.

Gianni laughed at that.

"Gianni? If you had something you cared about, and it broke?"

Gianni and I both still care about our stuffties, even if we don't want people to know about that secret. He knew I could mention what would make him cry—if it broke—so he quickly said, "Yeah, sure, Justin Case. True."

"Everybody cries sometimes," Bartholomew Wiggins said.

"Absolutely," Montana C. said.

"Everybody cries sometimes," Cash said in a *making fun of it* voice, and then added, "Justin Case is just standing up for his girlfriend, because he loves her. Justin and Pudding sittin' in a tree . . ."

"You know what?" I asked Cash, not fully knowing *what* myself, but just knowing for sure I did not want him to finish that dumb song.

"What?" Cash asked. "You love her?"

"I don't know anybody as interested in love as you, Cash. You are the most in-love-with-love kid I ever met."

He said, "You love her" a couple more times, but he stopped when people kept saying "in-love-with-love kid." Which is good because my only idea left was maybe I should punch him right on his nose.

~~~~~~

August 24, Tuesday

I punched Cash in the nose.

My fist pounded into the front of his face and smashed the whole thing into even more bits than Penelope Ann Murphy's ring. There was blood everywhere, running in rivers down his face and making gunky puddles all over the tennis court.

All the Hawks cheered. James/Jay even smiled, and then put a gold medal on a red-white-and-blue ribbon around my neck.

"You are the hero of Camp GoldenBrook," he said. "And my personal hero, too, Justin Krzeszewski."

I said, "Wait, you know how to pronounce my last name?"

Before he could answer, Gingy and Poopsie danced with my third-grade teacher Ms. Termini across the top of the pool, singing "The Star-Spangled Banner" very enthusiastically while Qwerty and my chewed-up knights played banjos together on a rainbow behind them.

Then I woke up and got ready for camp, where . . .

1. I didn't win any medals, or

2. punch any noses, and

3. no old people sang loud patriotic songs on the pool.

Unfortunately, sort of fortunately, and very fortunately.

∿∿∿∿∿

August 25, Wednesday

Today was the second-to-last day of Color War. Our second-to-last chance to catch those stinky Red Team kids who think they are so great.

I ate a healthy breakfast of disgusting gunk that Mom made when I asked for the healthiest thing possible and drank my whole glass of grapefruit juice even though grapefruit juice squinches my face very tight.

I am going to invent healthy food that tastes like gummy worms and become a millionaire when I am done with this whole camp thing.

The big event today was Obstacle Course. Obstacle Course means you have to do the terrible rings and not fall in the mud, which might have quicksand underneath it, but then you are not done yet. No way. That is not enough. Next you have to run down the big hill without tripping and then up the steps to the bridge. You have to go across the bridge very fast, but not running. Hopping. If your other foot touches the bridge planks, you have to go back to the beginning with everybody groaning and covering their faces in shame at you and then you have to start the hopping again. Then if you ever get to the other side of the bridge, you have to quickly pick up an egg out of a big blue bucket with a spoon and bring it to another big blue bucket across the field, without dropping it along the way. If you drop it, because you are trying to go faster to make up for lost time with the hopping and the quicksand delays, you get egg goo all over your sneakers. But too bad on you (okay, me) because you have to dash back all eggily to the first egg bucket, pick up a new egg, and please oh please try not to drop that one, too.

Then you have to do hurdles.

Hurdles are this thing that's like running but watch out because whoops, in your way there are—I am not even joking— metal fence parts. Which obviously you should just go around. But no. That is not true in camp. You have to somehow just jump right on over the fences. Like you are a cow and the fence is the moon.

As I was running toward the first hurdle, I was thinking about that nursery rhyme and why would people teach that to a kid? A cow can't jump over the moon. A cow can't jump over anything. There is so much kids need to learn in life, and they are new on the planet, so it is kind of mean to waste their time teaching them a cow jumps over the moon.

And then I crashed into the first hurdle. Like a cow, crashing into a, well, not a moon. A bush. A cow running across a field planning to jump over the moon, which no way can it do, and crashing into a bush. Or a metal fence.

And then not learning from its mistake.

Because I had to get up and run toward the next hurdle.

Or maybe it is called a hurt-all. Because, OW.

One of my feet cleared the next hurdle. The other foot knocked it down. I fell flat on my knees after the third hurdle. I lay there on the track, looking at it, at the little pebbles I had a very close-up view of, while I made my excellent plan: to not get up off the track.

I figured if I just stayed there long enough, it would turn to winter and I could sneak home because camp would be done.

But then I heard the foghorn voice of my counselor James/ Jay, and he was not saying, *Hey, Justin, are you okay? Let me help you up,* or anything nice like that. He was laughing.

Laughing because I fell down.

Laughing because I was lying on the track until winter.

That made my bottom teeth clench into a fist with my top teeth. I decided I would be bold, and mighty forces would come to my aid. I decided to pretend I was one of my unchewed knights and had superpowers of flying over hurdles and Feeling No Pain. I got up off the track, and with the horrible sound of that horrible counselor's horrible laughter clanging in my ears, I ran faster than ever toward the next hurdle.

And smashed into it.

I got up and ran toward the next one.

I got the first foot over and the second foot mostly over, but the darn thing caught the tip of my sneaker, and down I went again.

I only stayed on the track for a few seconds before I pushed myself up and charged at the second-to-last hurdle. Which I kind of ran around. And then there was only one hurdle between me and the finish line. No other hurdlers were running anymore. I was not sure if they had all finished or some had died on the track behind me. I ran as best I could with the whole bloody-bruised-body problem and jumped, well, into the hurdle.

It took some time to disentangle myself from it. I think I might have broken it, but I had to get across the finish line, so I stood up. Only one of my legs was bendy and the hurdle was attached to my shirt, so it had to come across the finish line with me. It clanked, or maybe that was just my damaged parts clanking.

When I got across the line, I fell down again, with the hurdle on top of me. And then the other kids were on top of me, too, yanking the hurdle off and laughing, but mostly I think laughing with me although I was very far from laughing myself. But still. Even some of the kids from the Red Team were crowding around me, like Xavier Schwartz, who said, "Justin Case is the most awesome hurdler EVER!"

Not Cash, though. What he said is, "Yeah, that's why we LOST. AGAIN." Then he kicked some rocks. He is the kind of kid who really, really hates losing. He stomped away toward the tennis courts.

While I was watching him go, Natalia asked if I was okay. I said yes, and then I didn't even go to the nurse, not just because I didn't want Cash to tease me for being a nurse-going baby as well as a terrible loser-hurdler but also because Montana C. was smiling at me. And then especially because she said to Natalia, "Justin just has no quit in him at all."

"True that," Natalia said back.

Which was not a gold medal and definitely didn't make Cash stop hating me, but still, it was pretty cool. I kept those words in my mind the whole rest of the day, and I was so busy enjoying those nice words that I hardly noticed my sore knees at all until I got home to my dog who had done about as well at doggie Obedience School as I had done at hurdles.

We talked about it in Dog for a while and then watched cartoons together.

〜〜〜〜〜

August 26, Thursday

The reason I dropped my camp bag on the lawn this morning is that just as I was about to get onto the camp bus, the bus farted really loud, right in my direction.

Montana C. saw. She laughed. She laughed the whole time I gathered up my stuff and climbed up the farty bus's steps

Pbbbbt.

and trudged down the aisle of high-backed bus seats, deciding where to sit, because obviously not with Montana C., who was laughing at me.

Until she said, "Hey, Justin Case! Come sit with me and tell me why that bus fart made you drop your stuff!"

"Because," I yelled back. "Bus farts are toxic!"

"Yeah," said some older kids in the back row. "They totally are. Toxic."

Some little kids I was passing giggled together, whispering, "Bus farts."

When I got to Montana C.'s seat, she said, "They are

toxic. But maybe they give you superpowers. Maybe you got turned into Bus Fart Man."

And it is possible she was right, because of what happened at the swim meet today and also the fact that the horrible flip-flops of doom stopped hurting my feet at all.

Well, the first thing that happened at the swim meet, which is apparently the Grande Finale of Color War, is that I came in second in backstroke.

I was swimming against Gianni Schicci and Bartholomew Wiggins and also Koji (who came in first), but still, I think the

combination of Bus Fart power and practicing backstroke all weekend, including the extra time after Gingy kicked Mr. Cranky Pants out of the pool, really made a difference.

I was sitting on the edge of the pool with my silver medal around my neck and my feet dangling in the water during the underwater swim competition. Next to me on one side was Koji, whose gold medal was the same size as my silver medal, so it's not a huge deal, just a different color, and Cash, who had two golds and a silver from his races. I still had cannonballing to come, I was telling myself; I might still get a gold if I could manage to do Poopsie's invention: the Super Dooper Big Boogie Boondoggle Splashmaster Cannonball. If I could just do that one awesome cannonball trick as well and splashy as I've been practicing it and Poopsie has been coaching me to do it all summer, it could be a medal winner, maybe even gold. And maybe that is the gold that will put the Blue Team over the top, and I could be the hero of Camp GoldenBrook after all. I was imagining myself being carried on everybody's shoulders, with everybody chanting, *JUSTIN, JUSTIN*, and maybe a few *Hooray for Justin*'s in there, too.

It was a happy imagining. And the sun was perfect on my

head, warm but gentle, and the pool area smelled like clean laundry. So everything was good.

But a bad feeling happened in my belly. At first, I wasn't sure why. I asked myself if maybe it was because I knew in reality that it was unlikely that people would carry me on their shoulders and even if they did I would probably fall off and crack my head open. *But no*, myself answered, *that is just reality. That is not the reason for my sick-belly feeling.*

I squinted harder into the pool. Montana C. was touching the wall at the far end of the pool, and she was smiling her great big Montana C. smile with droplets of water plinking off her eyelashes back into the pool. I almost smiled at her, but then I didn't because she is on the Red Team, and that is when I looked for the underwater racer from my team, the Blue Team, which was Penelope Ann Murphy.

I didn't see her. And then I did.

She was under the water. She was not coming up.

"Hey!" I shouted. "Penelope Ann Murphy is not coming up from under the water!"

"You are the most worried kid ever," somebody said to me, maybe Xavier—probably Xavier because he says that kind of thing about me a lot. But I can't be sure because I didn't look over there. I was looking at James/Jay.

"Save her!" I yelled at him.

"She's just joking around," James/Jay said, rolling his eyes.

"She's not," I said. "She might not be!" I stood up on the edge of the pool.

"You go in, your team is disqualified," James/Jay said.

I threw off my medal. It clonked Cash on the head. "Hey," he growled.

"I think maybe she's not kidding," I said to him, and I dived into the pool.

I didn't really have a plan. I never got the pennies off the floor of the pool, so there was pretty little chance I could get a whole Penelope Ann Murphy up from there. But I kicked harder than Gingy even kicked at Mr. Cranky Pants and aimed for Penelope Ann Murphy, blinking my stinging eyes that had never been open underwater before.

Cash zoomed past me, but not by much. We got to Penelope Ann Murphy at about the same second, right after two grown-ups got there. We all grabbed parts of Penelope Ann

and yanked her by the armpits and the kneepits up and up and up.

I burst through the ceiling of water into the air. I gulped my biggest, most delicious mouthful of air of my whole life. Then I gulped a few more while my overcooked-spaghetti legs flopped a lot less powerfully than a few seconds earlier but enough to get my portion of Penelope Ann Murphy over to the edge of the pool just a few seconds after the part that Cash and the grown-ups, who it turned out were the lifeguards, were dragging.

Before that second, I had never seen the lifeguards do anything but wear sunglasses, blow whistles, and point.

Turns out, they have other skills, too. They dragged Penelope Ann out of the pool and did stuff to her until she coughed and maybe even puked on the concrete.

For the first time all summer, everybody cheered for her.

Cash and I were still in the pool. We rested on our forearms on the edge. He squinted at me with one of his blue eyes shut, just like the leader of my bad-guy knights, Steeltrap.

"Sorry," I told him. "Guess I lost us another one."

Cash shrugged. "Whatevs," he said. "Cool rescue."

I smiled. "Yeah," I said.

We didn't end up getting disqualified. We got thanked by Eddie, the head of the whole camp. James/Jay got talked to—and not in a complimenting way. In a *What the heck is wrong with you, and you are not welcome back at camp next summer, you mean counselor you* kind of way.

Cash and I watched that whole thing happen. Cash said, "He was a bad counselor anyway."

"Yeah," I said. "Hey, so, was his name James or Jay?"

"Jake," Cash said.

"Oh," I said. "Jake? Really?"

"You kidding?" Cash asked.

But I didn't answer because Mike was calling my name to come back to the pool for the Cannonball Event.

I stood at the edge of the pool picturing Poopsie in his huge scuba goggles, and that made me giggle a little. I closed my eyes, took a deep breath, and decided to be bold. I did the Super Dooper Big Boogie Boondoggle Splashmaster Cannonball, and mighty forces came to my aid. It was the best I ever did it, including all the hundreds of splashy practices.

I got the Gold.

~~~~~~

August 27, Friday

Last day.

Penelope Ann Murphy didn't come to camp. I had made a decision in my mind on the bus that I would give her my perfect shell. Thinking of that made me almost start to cry. Of course not all the way to tears or anything. It's just, it is my perfect shell. How often does a person get something perfect? But my answer on the inside of me to that question was maybe Penelope had a really hard summer and nothing perfect to hold, even in her memory. So maybe she should have my shell.

But luckily she was absent, so I did not have to do that generous thing.

The other good thing that happened was all day we just basically played. There were lots of ice-cream sandwiches and do whatever you wants and an extra Quad in the middle of the day to sing the silliest songs and get up and do silly dances, which everybody did, even the boys, even the counselors. Natalia danced with Mike a few times. Then she danced for a second with me. That turned my legs into dough, so I had to rest up a little.

Then it was time to settle down for the prizes. It's not like Rec Soccer where everybody gets a prize, there's just a big plaque that hangs in the social hall from then on forever of who won Color War.

Red Team won.

"Whatevs," I said to Cash, who was leaning back on his hands on the towel next to mine.

He smiled at me. "Yeah," he said.

I smiled back. Because, well, everybody says Yeah to Cash, and there he was saying it to me instead of me Getting It for losing Color War for him.

"We'll get 'em next year," he said.

"Maybe," I said instead of yeah. But what I was thinking was . . .

1. I am going to Science Camp next year. Not quitting is one thing. Signing up again is just nuts.
2. Is Cash not going back to Tennessee?
3. Oh, no.

~~~~~~

August 28, Saturday

I threw the horrible flip-flops of doom in the garbage can. Not the one in the kitchen, the one in the garage.

Ahhhhhhhhhhhh.

~~~~~~

August 29, Sunday

Mom and Dad are proud about my gold medal and also my two silvers. (They stopped asking about that other one from Montana C., which is hiding in my desk drawer. I am going to sneak it into her backpack sometime during fourth grade.)

But they are even prouder of how I handled camp and how I rose to the occasion.

They talked to me about it privately, just the three of us out on the deck. Natalia had called them, I guess. I don't know exactly what she told them because I was trying to hurry the conversation along and get to the next thing, which was a wrapped box sitting there waiting patiently on the table with the name JUSTIN on it. So I was not fully listening to every word, even though they were mostly words like *proud* and *brave,* which I do enjoy. But it was worth hurrying through those excellent words, it turned out.

In the box was a half-pound bag of gummy worms all for myself that I don't even have to share with anybody, not even Elizabeth.

Then after she got back from trying to walk Qwerty all by herself, Elizabeth told us the whole story of that adventure and then went dashing up to her room to get something. When she came back onto the deck, she handed me a heavy thing wrapped in tissue paper.

"What is it?" I asked. It was not my birthday, so I felt kind of confused.

"Open it," she said.

I took the tissue paper off it carefully. Underneath was a big papier-mâché item, painted in every imaginable color and a few others, too.

"Wow," I said.

"It's a battlefield," she said. "For your knights. I know they are just plastic toys, but I also know, well, they're . . . they need a field to battle on, to prove their hero-ness."

"Heroism," Dad said.

"Hero-ness" Elizabeth insisted, and pointed at the battlefield I was holding in my hands. "Heroes need a place to prove themselves, so they can get brave."

"Yeah," I told her.

"Well, that's what I was thinking, and I already made a million things for Mom and Dad, so why not you? And also it was going to be a bowl for your shell, but it smooshed so, oh, well."

"It's perfect," I whispered to her. And it was the truth.

So that is why just now, while everybody is sleeping, I just snuck into Elizabeth's room and arranged on her desk a little turret made of about 20 to 23 gummy worms, surrounding my shell. And next to it, I wrote a note that says, "For Elizabeth. Love, your brother, Justin K."

My heart is pounding now but partly in a proud way.

~~~~~~

August 30, Monday

What I love about summer is the nothing-to-do-ness of it.

Today I spent all morning digging a hole in the backyard, just for the fun of digging. Then I spent all afternoon undigging it, just for the fun of not getting yelled at anymore about what the heck I was doing digging up the whole darn garden, young man.

Elizabeth spent the day making a castle out of shoe boxes and construction paper for her perfect shell to be the queen of. (Elizabeth thinks the shell is a she.)

Qwerty spent the day throwing up the gummy worms that were originally guarding the shell on Elizabeth's desk.

Then at dinner out on the deck, Mom said to me that my friend named Cassius Plotz would like to play together sometime, and I said, "Who is Cassius Plotz," and Mom said his mother called and said you were his best friend at camp this summer and I said, "Cash?"

So he is coming over for a playdate on Thursday.

I am trying to think *whatevs*, but instead I am actually thinking *Oh, no.*

∿∿∿∿

August 31, Tuesday

Today is the last day of August. When we got home from another morning at the pool, all red-eyed and cloggy-eared, the class lists were in the mailbox. Elizabeth tore hers open, shouting, "I'm in the grades! No more kindergarten! Finally in the grades!"

But I've been in the grades a long time, so I was much less sparky about the whole thing. Fourth grade sounds soooo much older than third, never mind first. I opened my envelope carefully, after I put my stuff in the laundry and went to the kitchen. I am not so uncontrolled as first grade.

Fourth grade.

That is the good news.

The rest, I decided, is just a disaster that I am not going to think about yet because it is still summer for goodness' sake.

But then I stared at the paper with my class list on it for a very long minute, because I could not stop thinking, *No way, no way.* While Elizabeth and Mom went upstairs to put her class list up on her new bulletin board, I got a pencil out of the everything drawer and sat down at the kitchen table with my list. I am more of a math guy than a decorate-a-bulletin-board guy, so I put a number from one to five next to each kid's name with one meaning *disaster* all the way up to five for *hooray*.

There was only one *hooray*.

There were a LOT of *disasters*.

And one zero next to Mr. Leonard, my fourth-grade teacher.

I am not being prejudiced, but I never had a man teacher before. A lot of people think he is cool because he has a quiet voice and his eyebrows can move independently of each other, especially if a kid says a wrong answer. No yelling, no putting your name on the board. Just an eyebrow, up a millimeter toward his hair. I don't know if it matters if it's the left eyebrow or the right that goes up. How am I supposed to know that? I am probably going to get at least one raised eyebrow in the first week, if I know me. Also, Mr. Leonard is a very tall person for a teacher, which means you have to tip your head back very far to see if one of his eyebrows went up, to know if you made a mistake. Which could give you a stiff neck.

I am actually used to having teachers who are female and more on the loud and obvious side of letting you know when

you are incorrect. But now I got Mr. Leonard and his eyebrows for a fourth-grade teacher.

I also got Xavier and Noah, Montana C. and Daisy in my class. Not Penelope Ann Murphy or Bartholomew Wiggins but, even worse, a kid with the name of Cassius Plotz.

So fourth grade is probably going to be a complete disaster.

But right now, it is still August, so I after I erased all the scores I gave out—so nobody would be able to know my opinions—I crumpled that class list up and threw it in the garbage in the kitchen. I poked it down into a bunch of gross breakfast garbage. I am not in the mood today for anybody to talk to me about how it's important to be brave and have a good attitude.

The mighty forces can come to my aid tomorrow.

For now, I am just going to sit here on the deck in my bare feet with their too much space between the toes while my knights battle it out on their lumpy battlefield. I can hear little shrieks of delight from Elizabeth's bedroom window, blending in with the birds across the yard, shrieking their delight to each other. Maybe they are in the grades, too.

What I am mostly doing is smelling the afternoon. I'm sucking today into my lungs as much as possible, because tomorrow when I breathe, it will be September air clogging up my respiratory system instead. And I just think it might be nice to have some summer left over inside me for if I need it.

August air in my backyard smells nothing like pudding or bus farts.

It smells like grass and heat and the sweet-sour of fresh gummy worms and also like Nothing to Worry About at all.